MERMAID DAYS™

A New Friend

Read more MERMAID DAYS™ books!

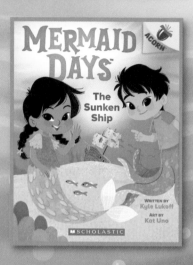

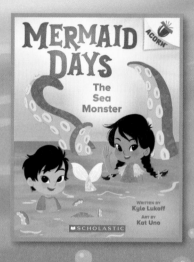

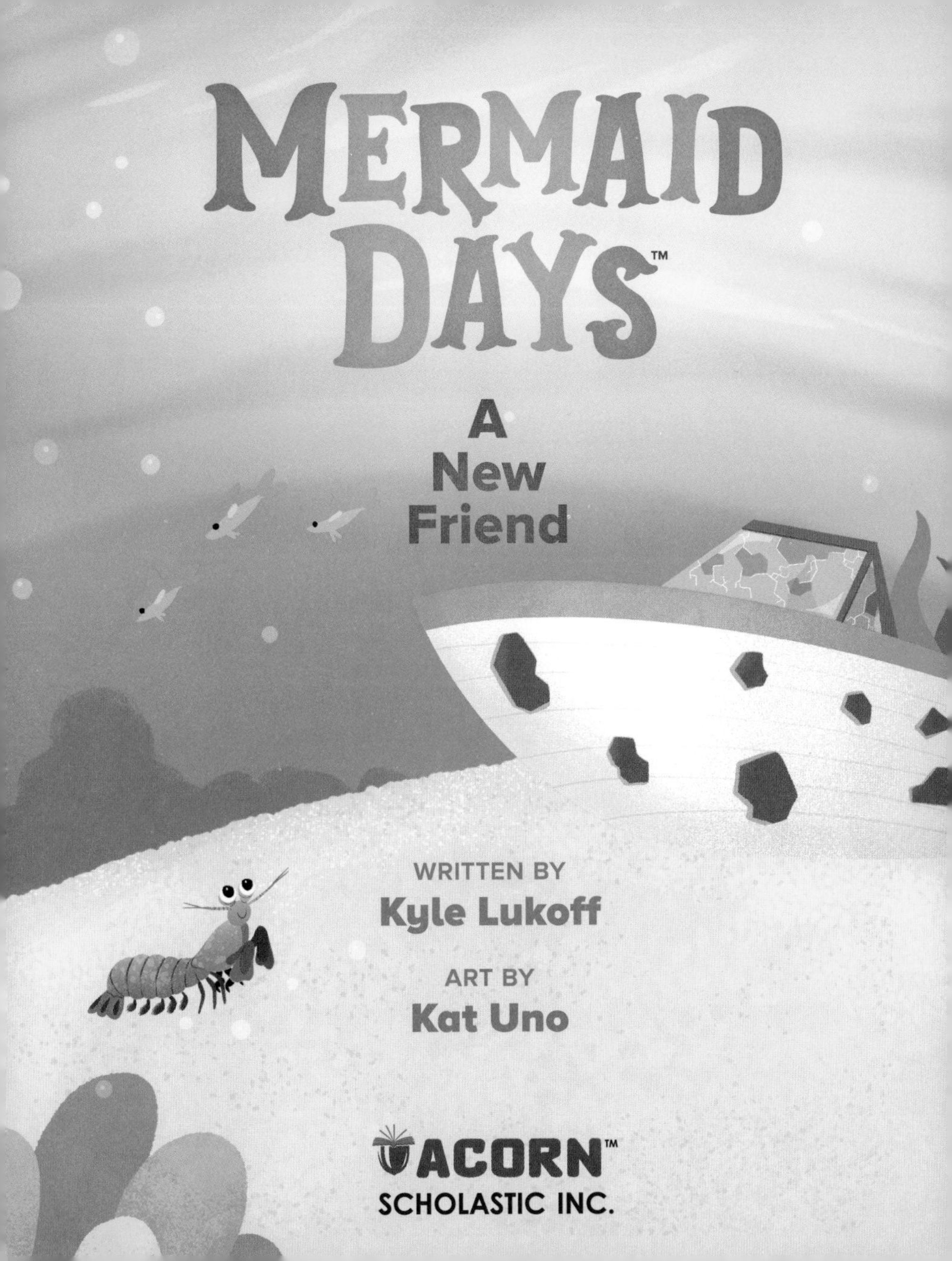

MERMAID DAYS™

A New Friend

WRITTEN BY
Kyle Lukoff

ART BY
Kat Uno

ACORN™
SCHOLASTIC INC.

For Olympia Bruce
—**KL**

Thank you to all the little readers who I hope enjoy this book!
—**KU**

Text copyright © 2023 by Kyle Lukoff
Illustrations copyright © 2023 by Kat Uno

Library of Congress Cataloging-in-Publication Data

Names: Lukoff, Kyle, author. | Uno, Kat, illustrator.
Title: A new friend / written by Kyle Lukoff; art by Kat Uno.
Description: First edition. | New York : Acorn/Scholastic Inc., 2023. |
Series: Mermaid days; 3 | Audience: Ages 4–6. | Audience: Grades K–1. |
Summary: When mermaid Vera and Octo-boy Beaker investigate what seems like a wave of vandalism in Tidal Grove, they discover a baby Mantis shrimp who does not fully understand his own power, and help him find his family.
Identifiers: LCCN 2022021157 | ISBN 9781338794977 (paperback) |
ISBN 9781338794984 (library binding)
Subjects: LCSH: Mermaids—Juvenile fiction. | Marine animals—Juvenile fiction. | Friendship—Juvenile fiction. | CYAC: Mermaids—Fiction. | Marine animals—Fiction. | Friendship—Fiction. | BISAC: JUVENILE FICTION / Readers / Beginner | JUVENILE FICTION / Mermaids & Mermen | LCGFT: Picture books.
Classification: LCC PZ7.L8456 Ne 2023 | DDC [E]—dc23
LC record available at https://lccn.loc.gov/2022021157

10 9 8 7 6 5 4 3 2 1   23 24 25 26 27

Printed in China   62
First edition, September 2023
Edited by Rachel Matson
Designed by Jaime Lucero

TABLE OF CONTENTS

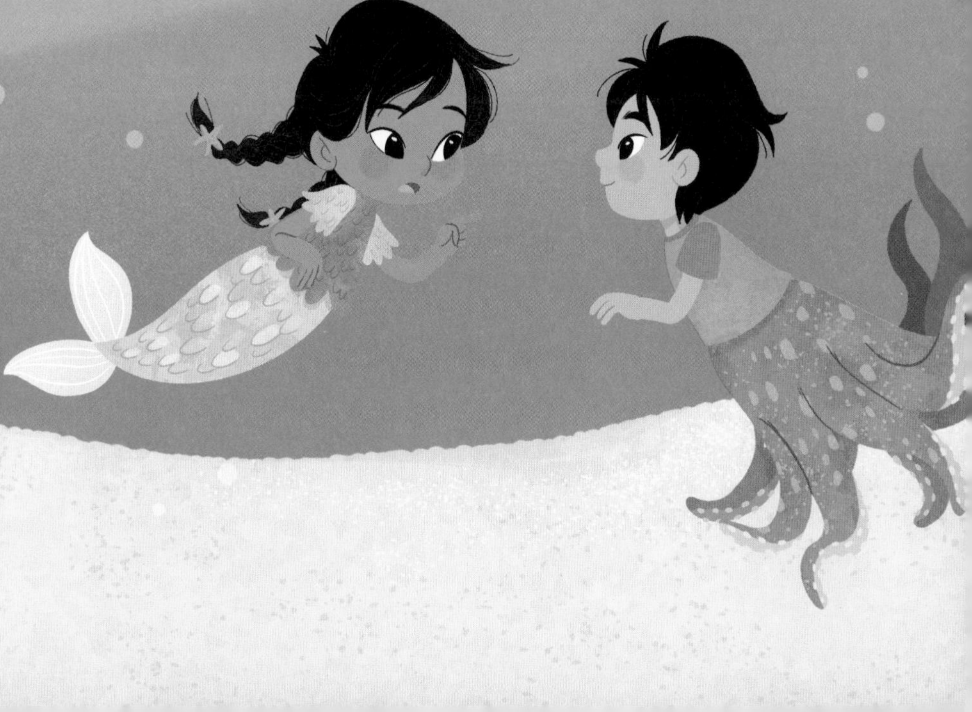

WHO LIVES IN TIDAL GROVE?

Vera

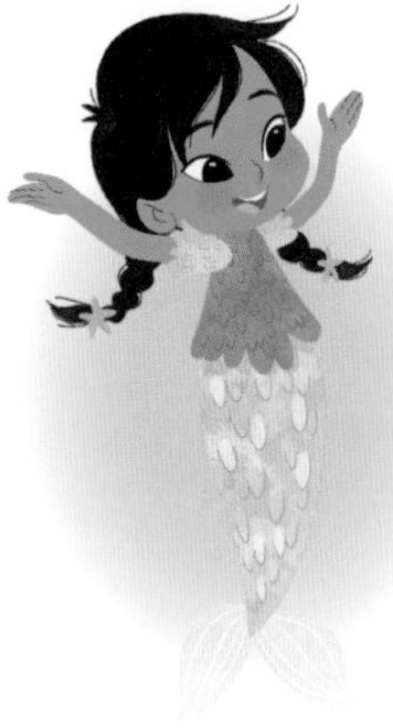

Beaker

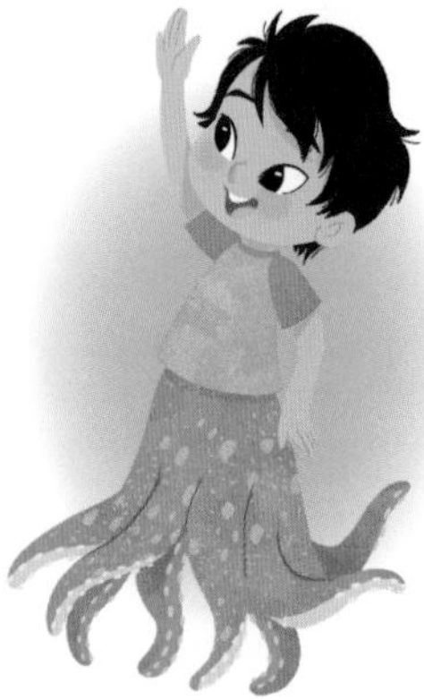

Beaker's Legs

Mr. Burbles

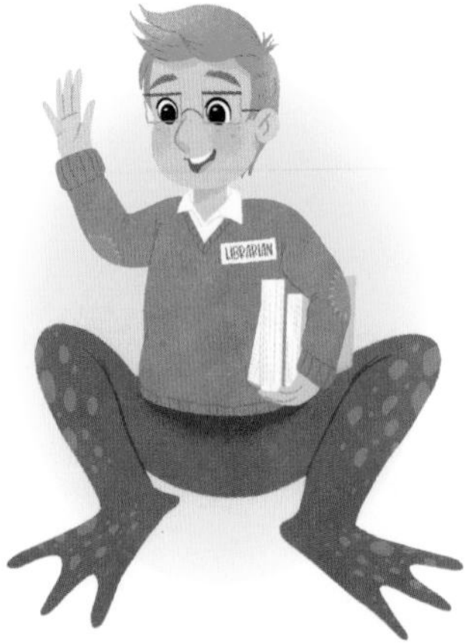
LIBRARIAN

Kelpie

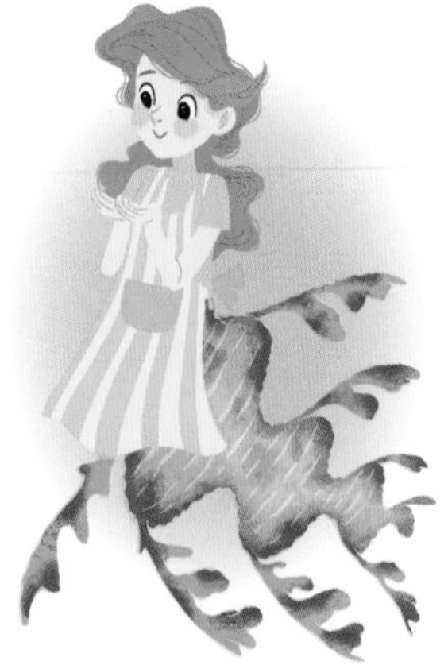

Baby Mantis Shrimp

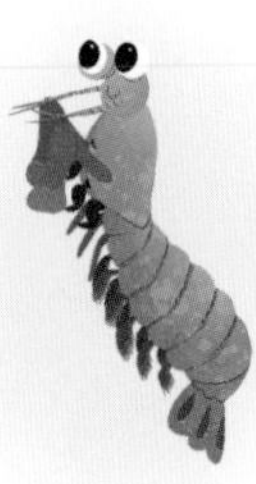

LOST AND FOUND

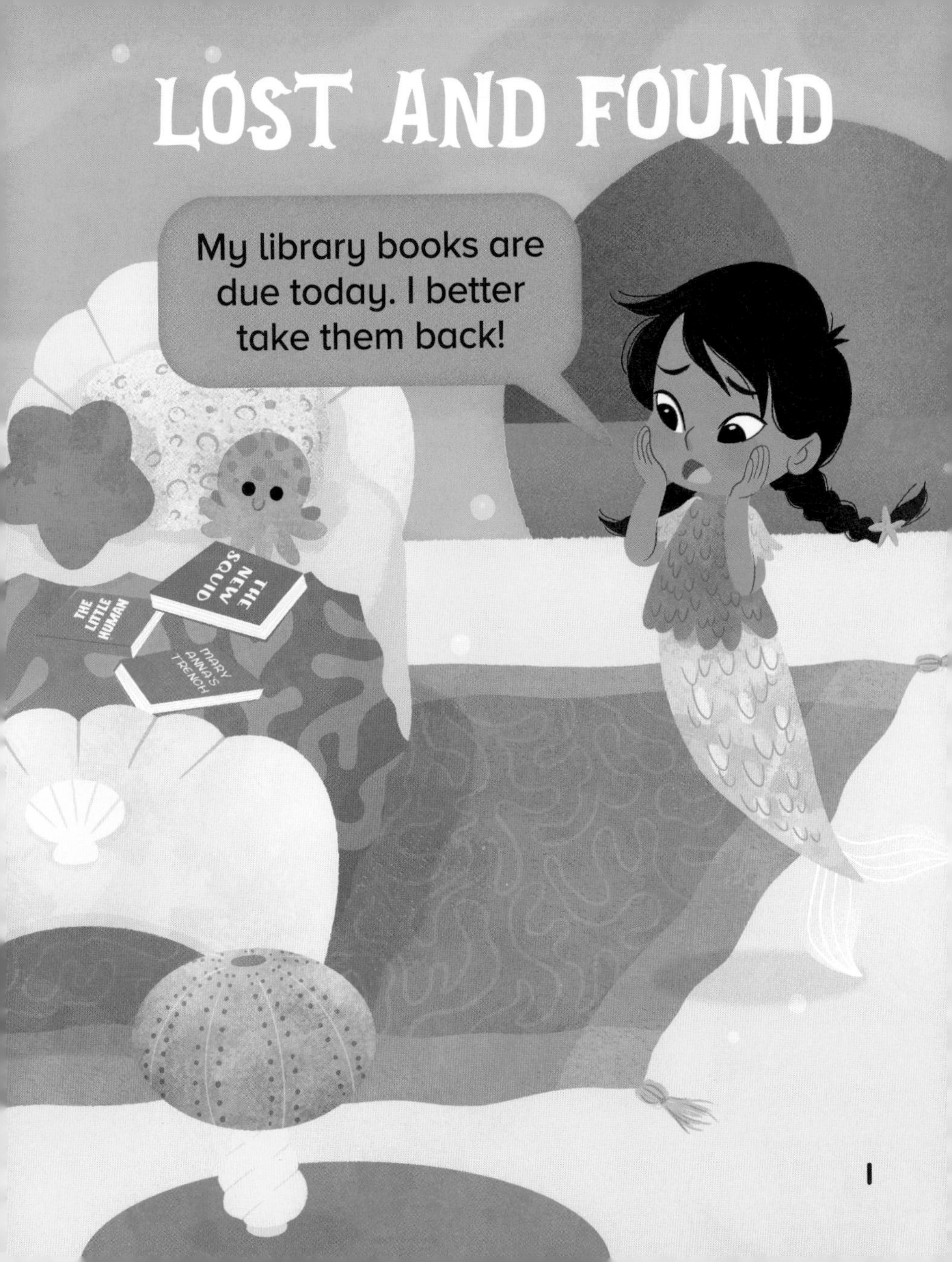
My library books are due today. I better take them back!
THE NEW SQUID
THE LITTLE HUMAN
MARY ANNA'S TRENCH

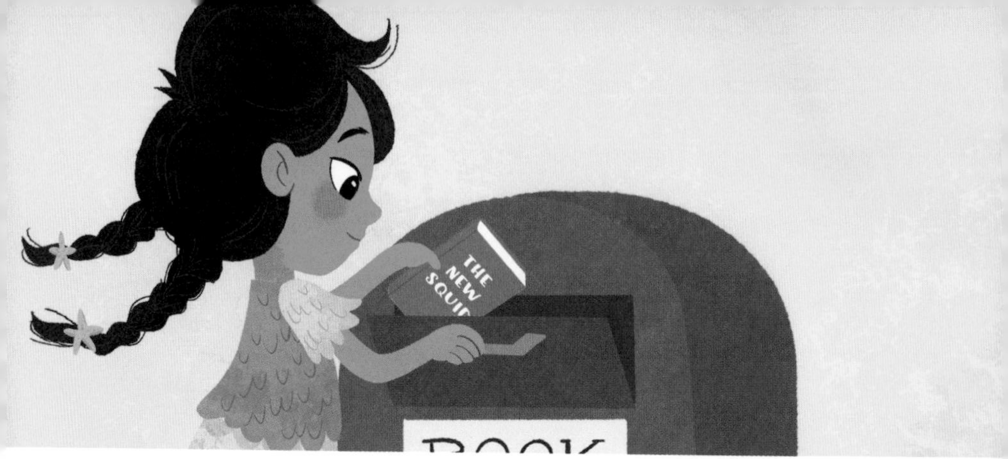

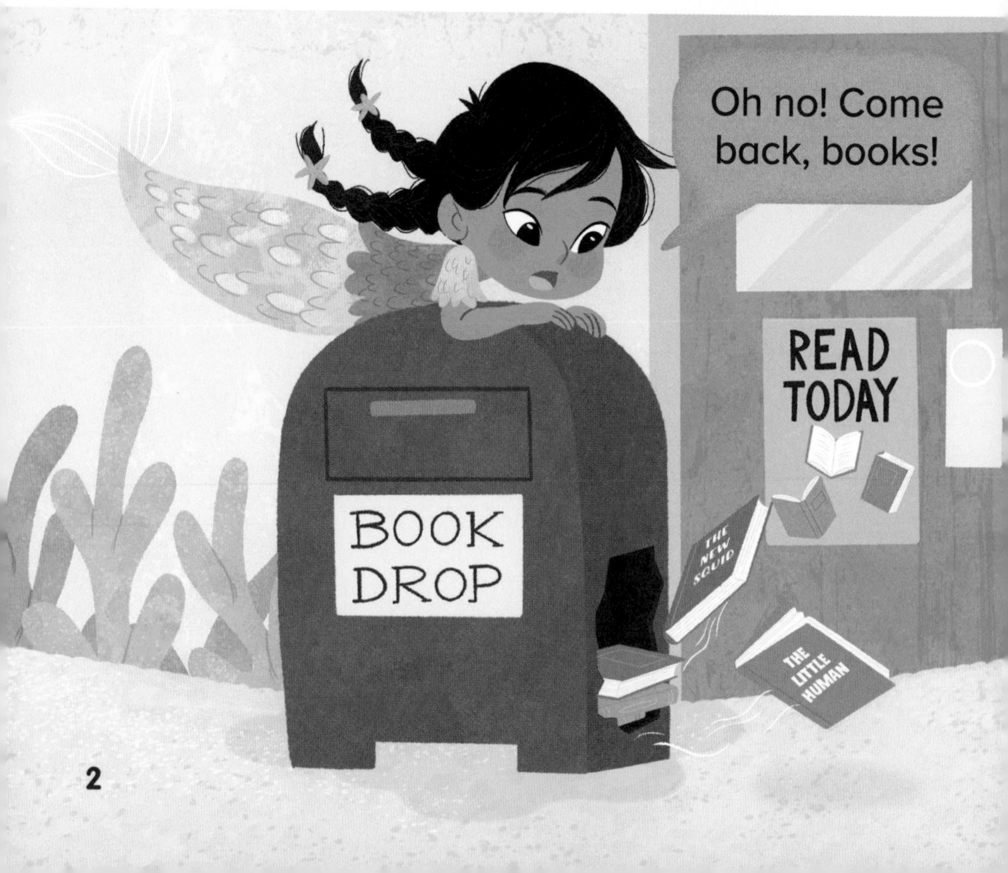
Oh no! Come back, books!
READ TODAY
BOOK DROP
THE NEW SQUID
THE LITTLE HUMAN

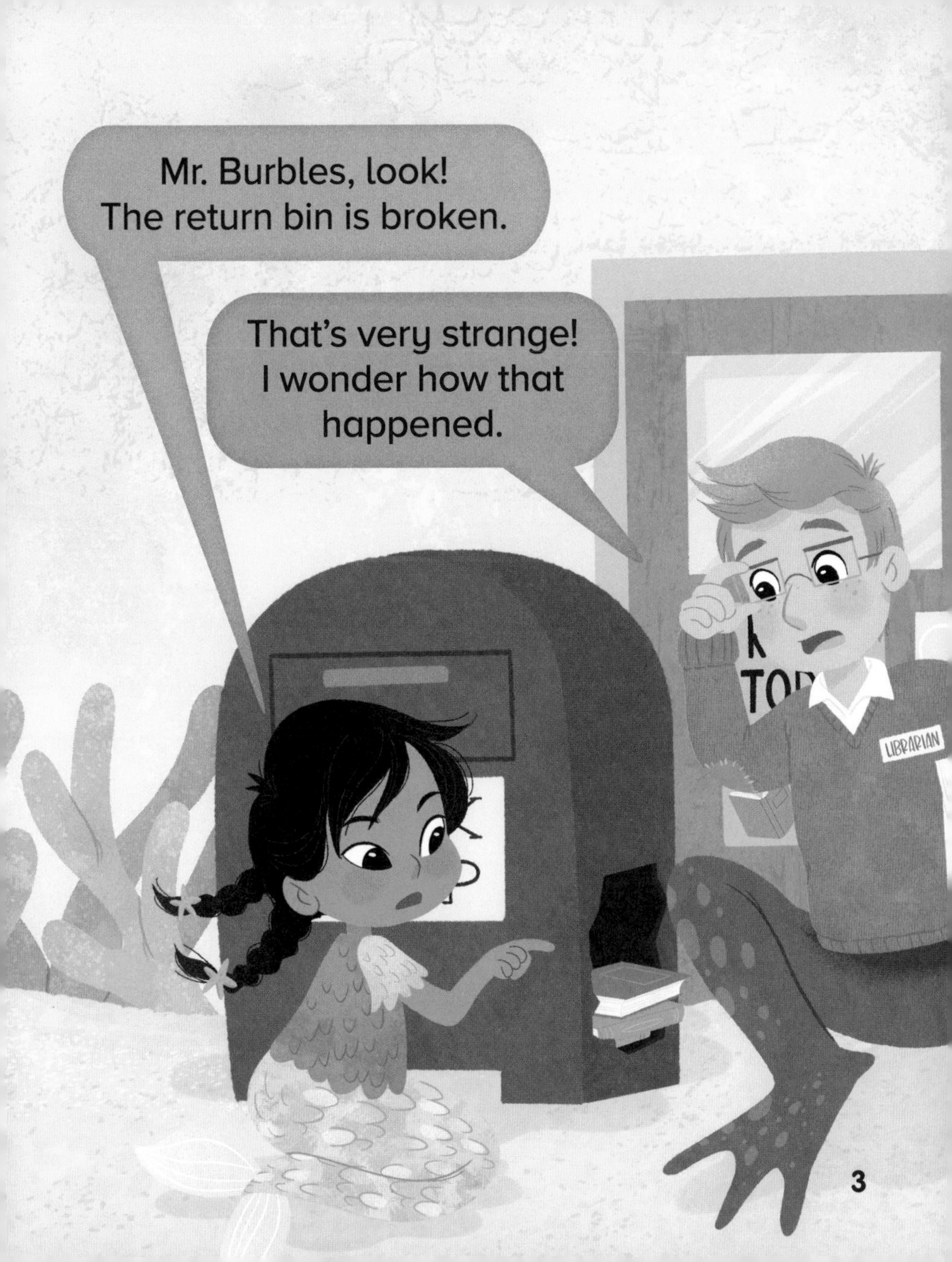
Mr. Burbles, look! The return bin is broken.
That's very strange! I wonder how that happened.
LIBRARIAN

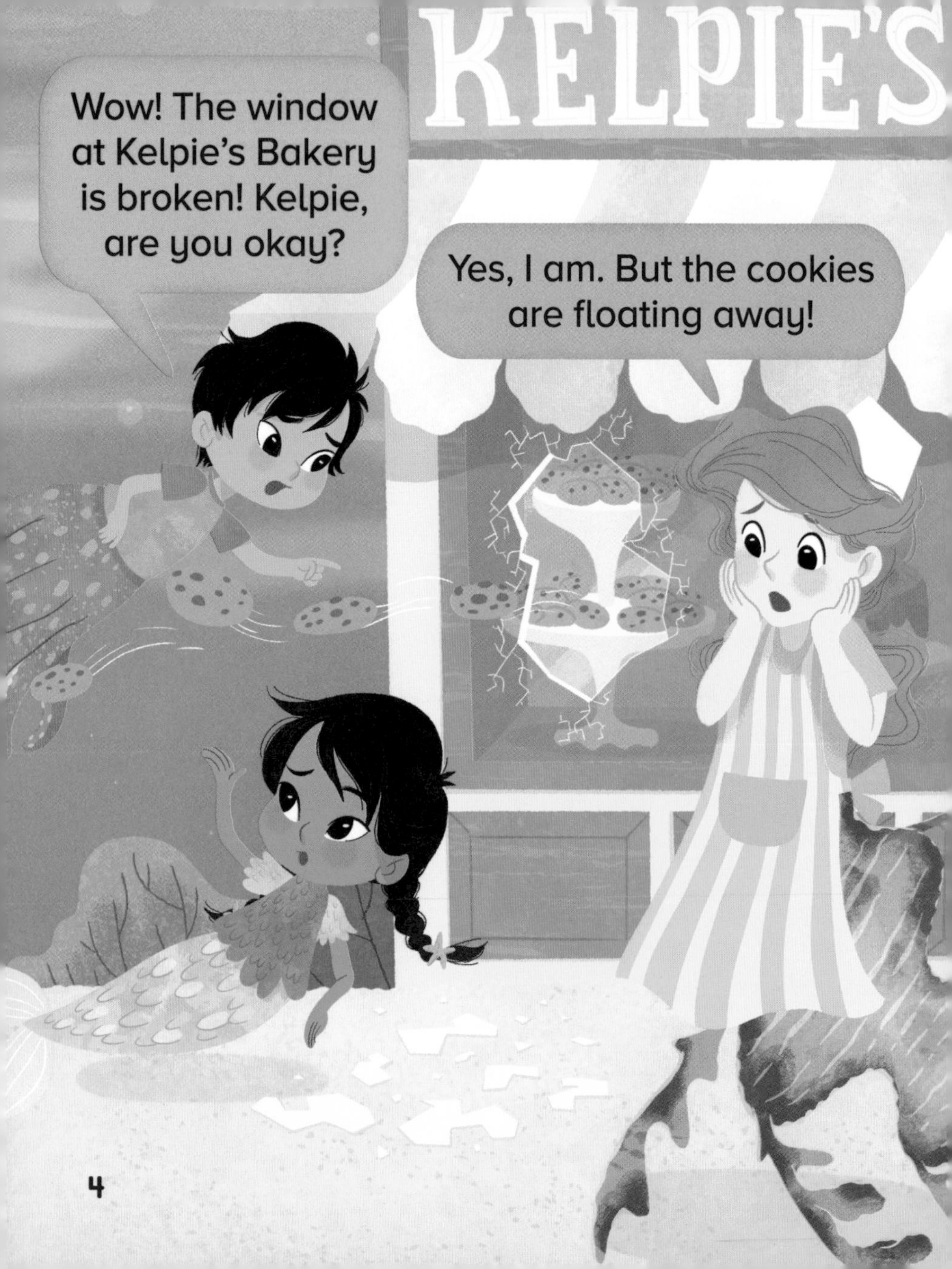
KELPIE'S
Wow! The window at Kelpie's Bakery is broken! Kelpie, are you okay?
Yes, I am. But the cookies are floating away!

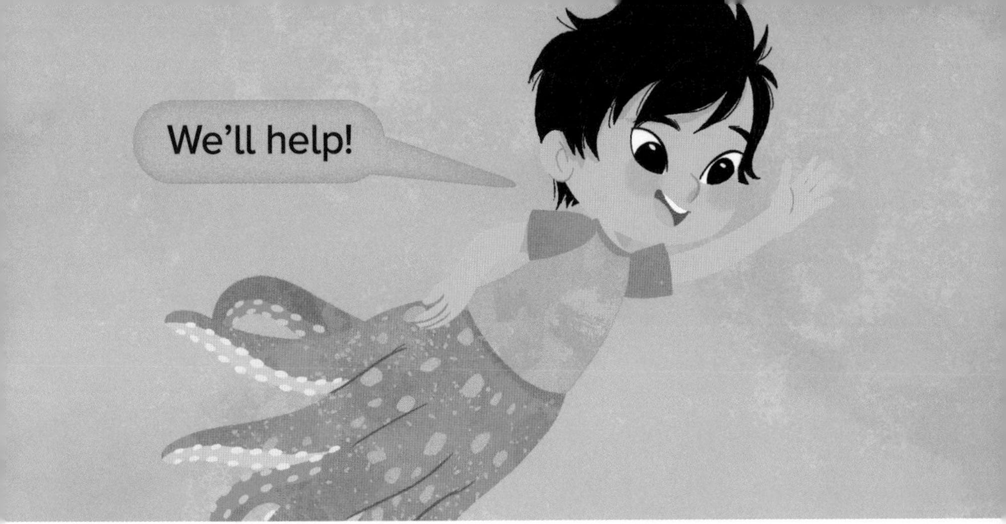
We'll help!

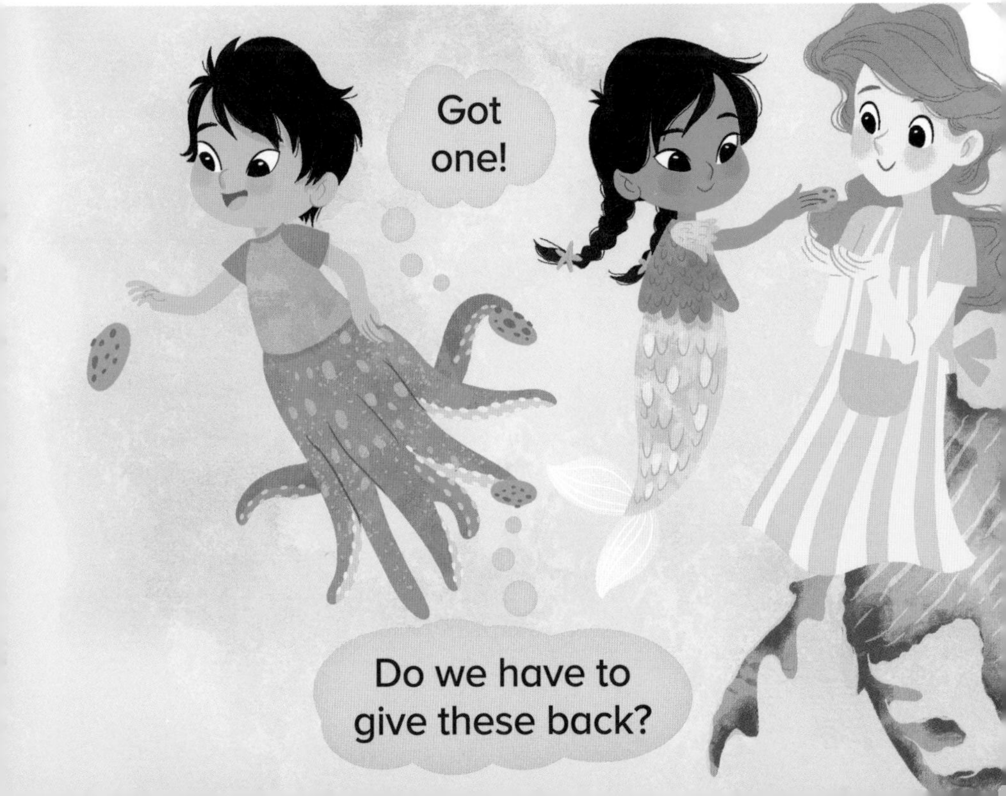
Got one!
Do we have to give these back?

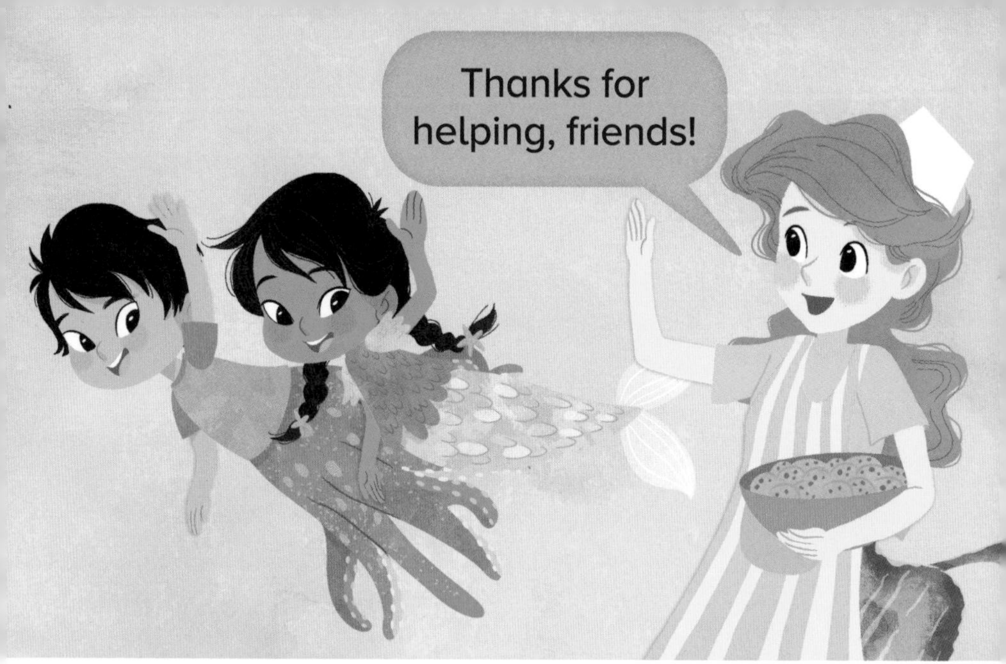
Thanks for helping, friends!

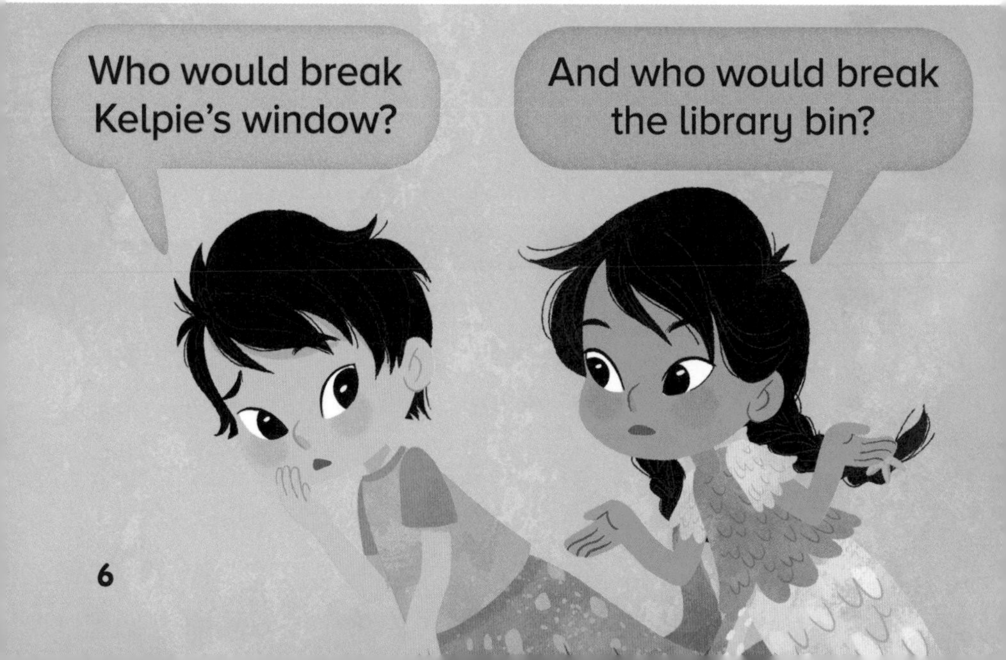
Who would break Kelpie's window?
And who would break the library bin?

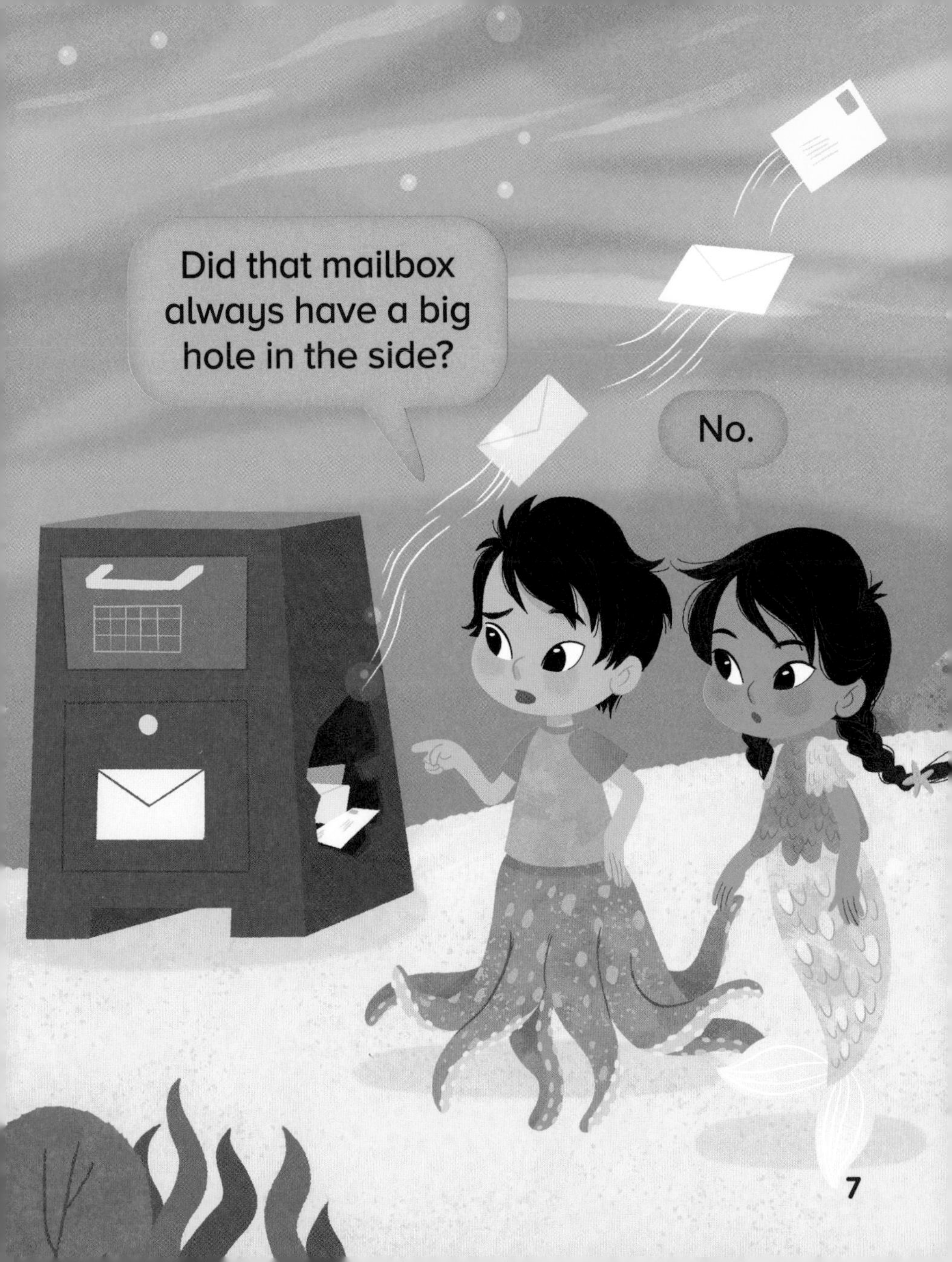
Did that mailbox always have a big hole in the side?
No.

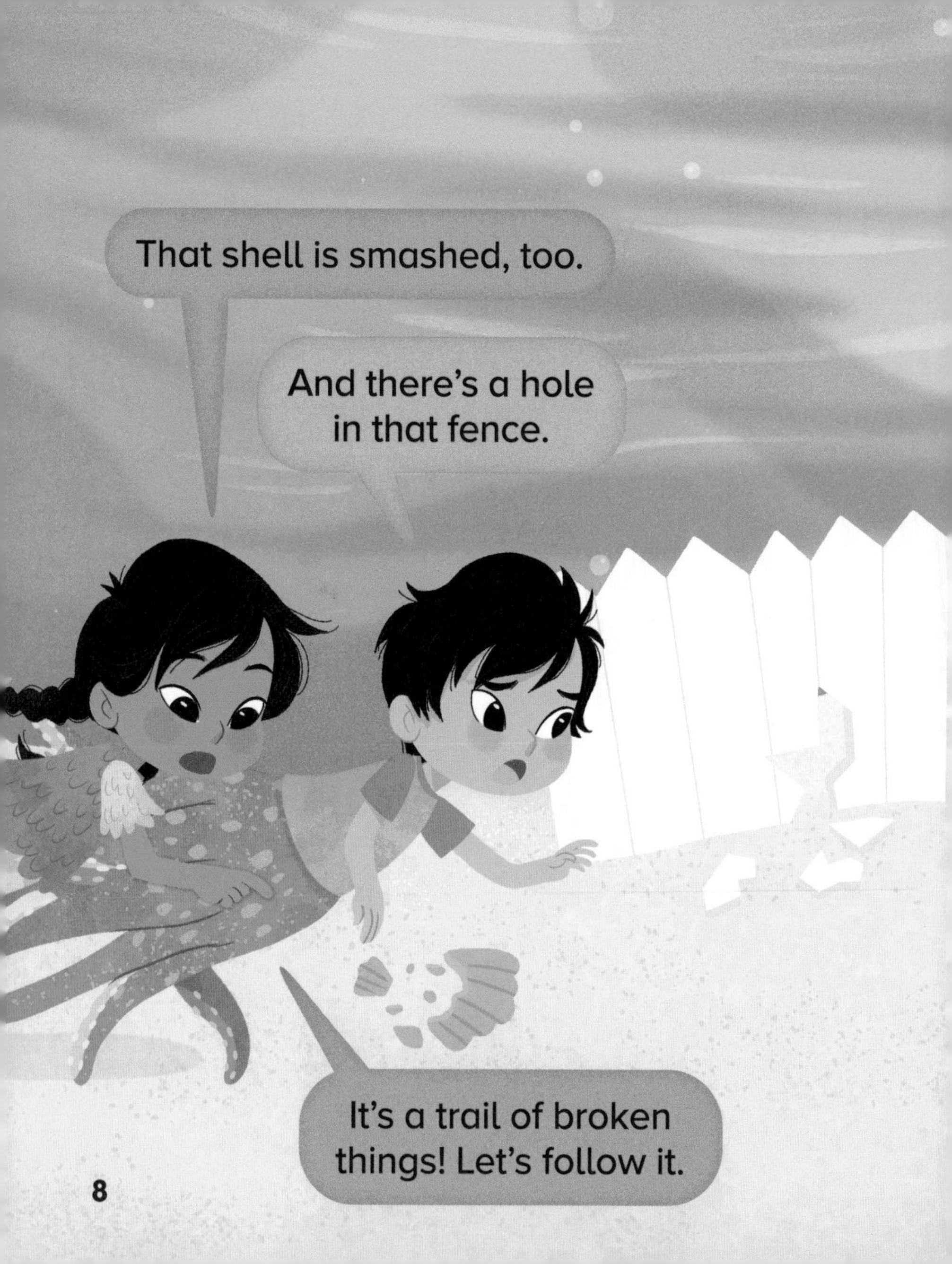
That shell is smashed, too.
And there's a hole in that fence.
It's a trail of broken things! Let's follow it.

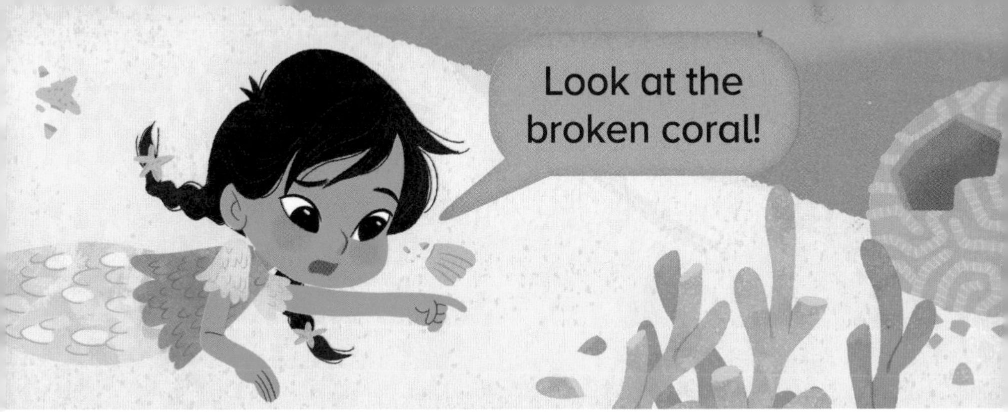
Look at the broken coral!

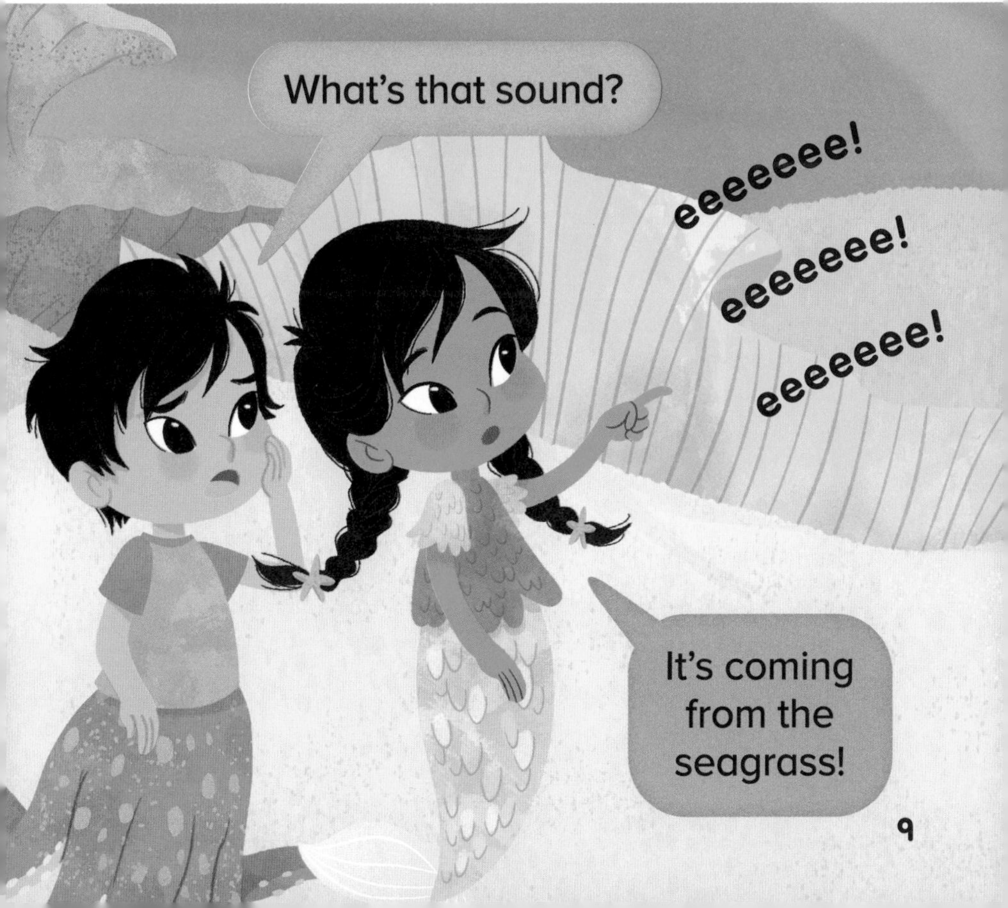
What's that sound?
eeeeeee!
eeeeeee!
eeeeeee!
It's coming from the seagrass!

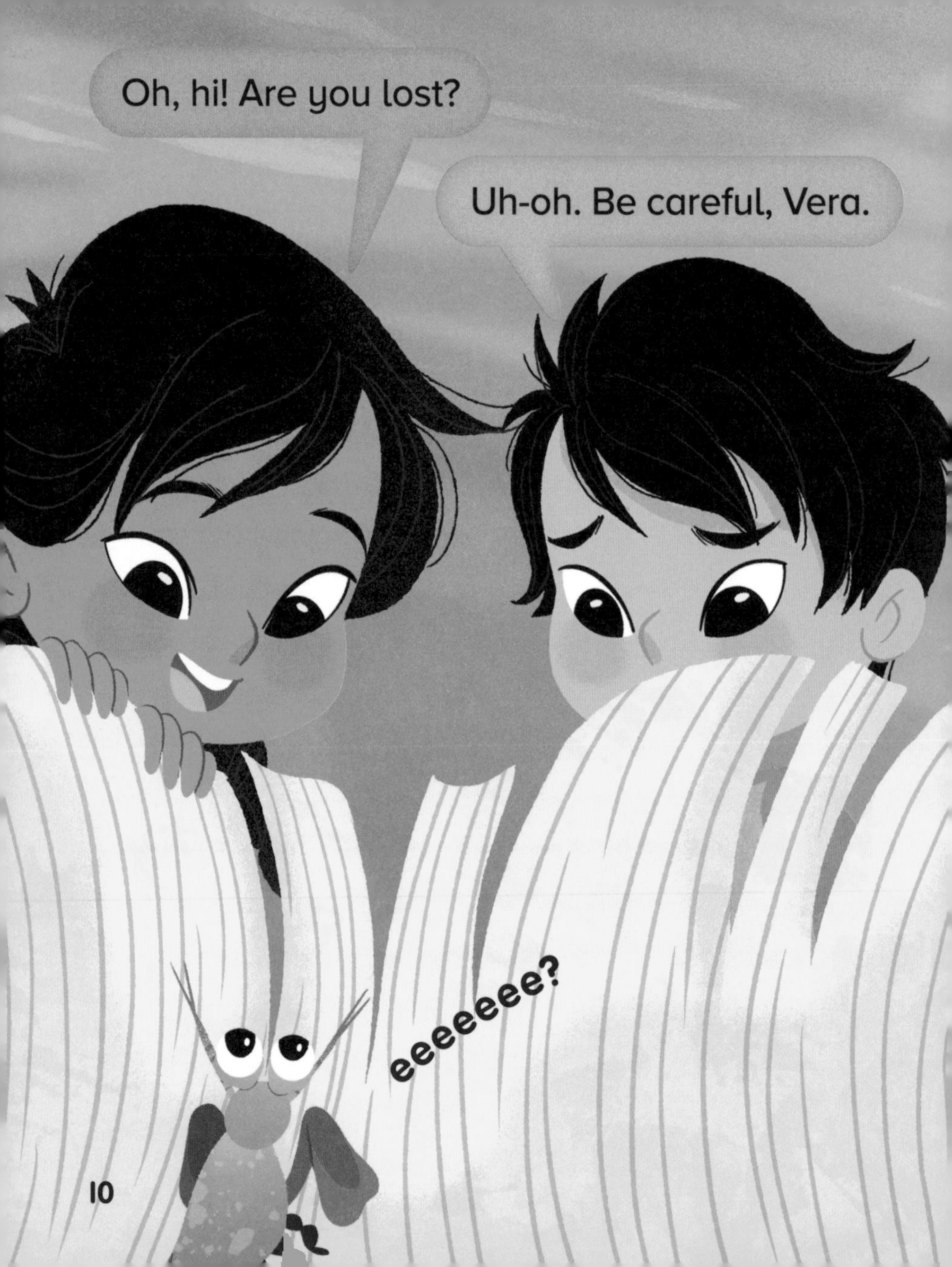
Oh, hi! Are you lost?
Uh-oh. Be careful, Vera.
eeeeeee?

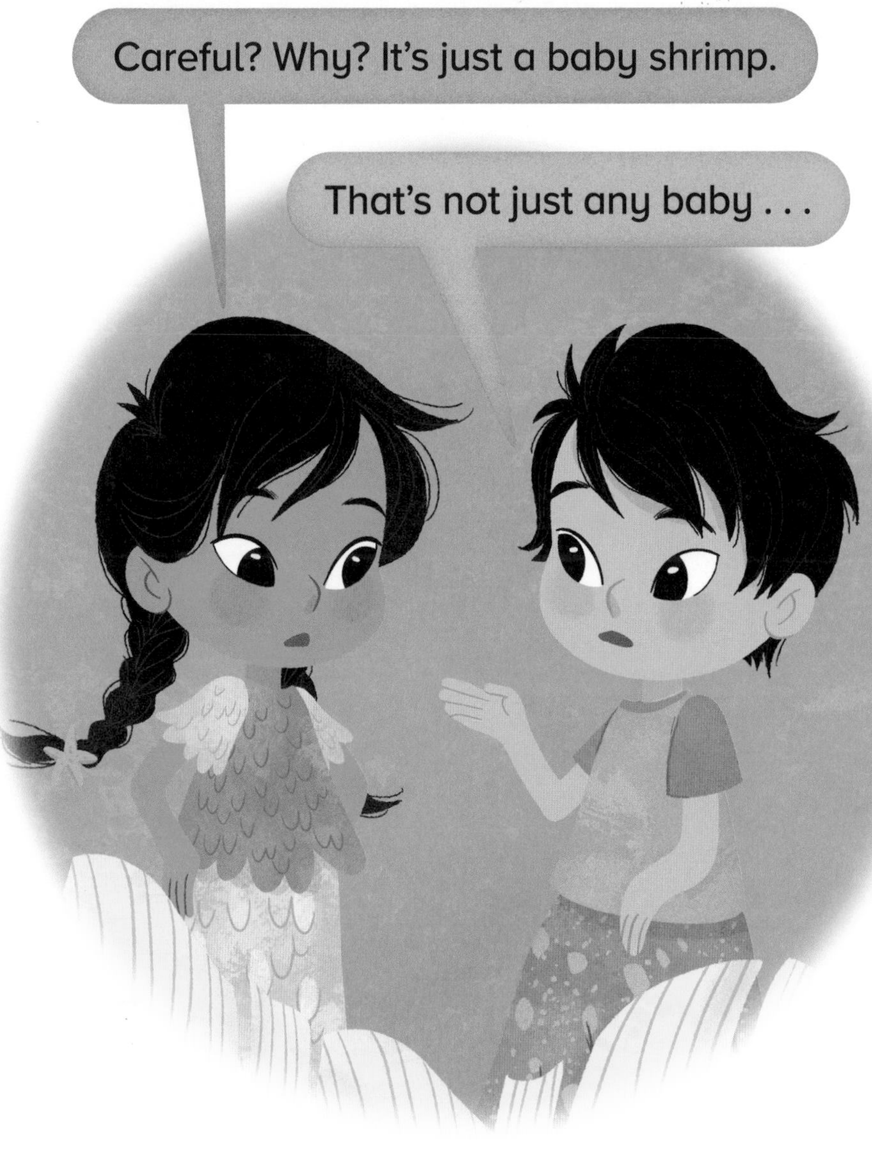
Careful? Why? It's just a baby shrimp.
That's not just any baby . . .

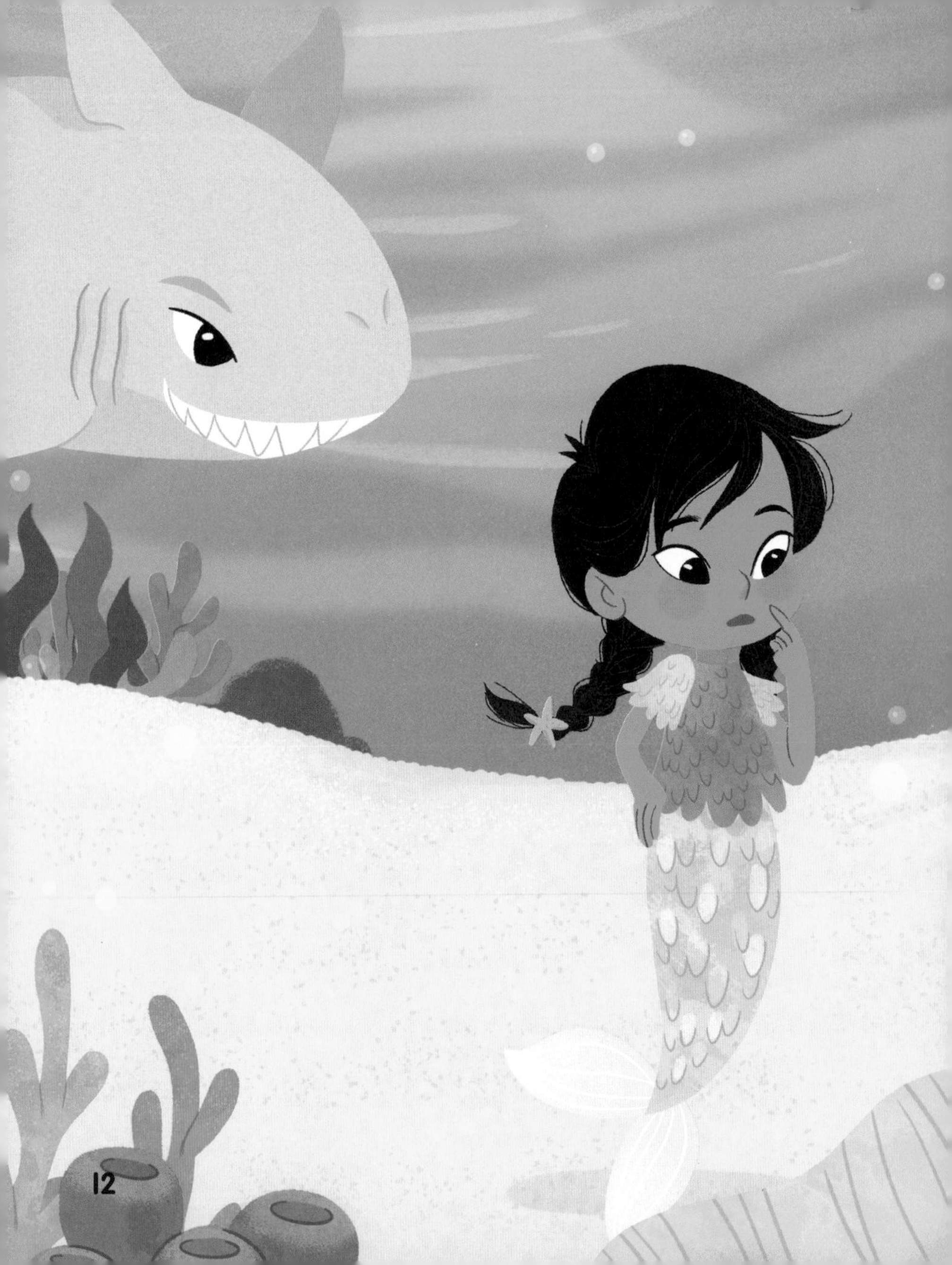

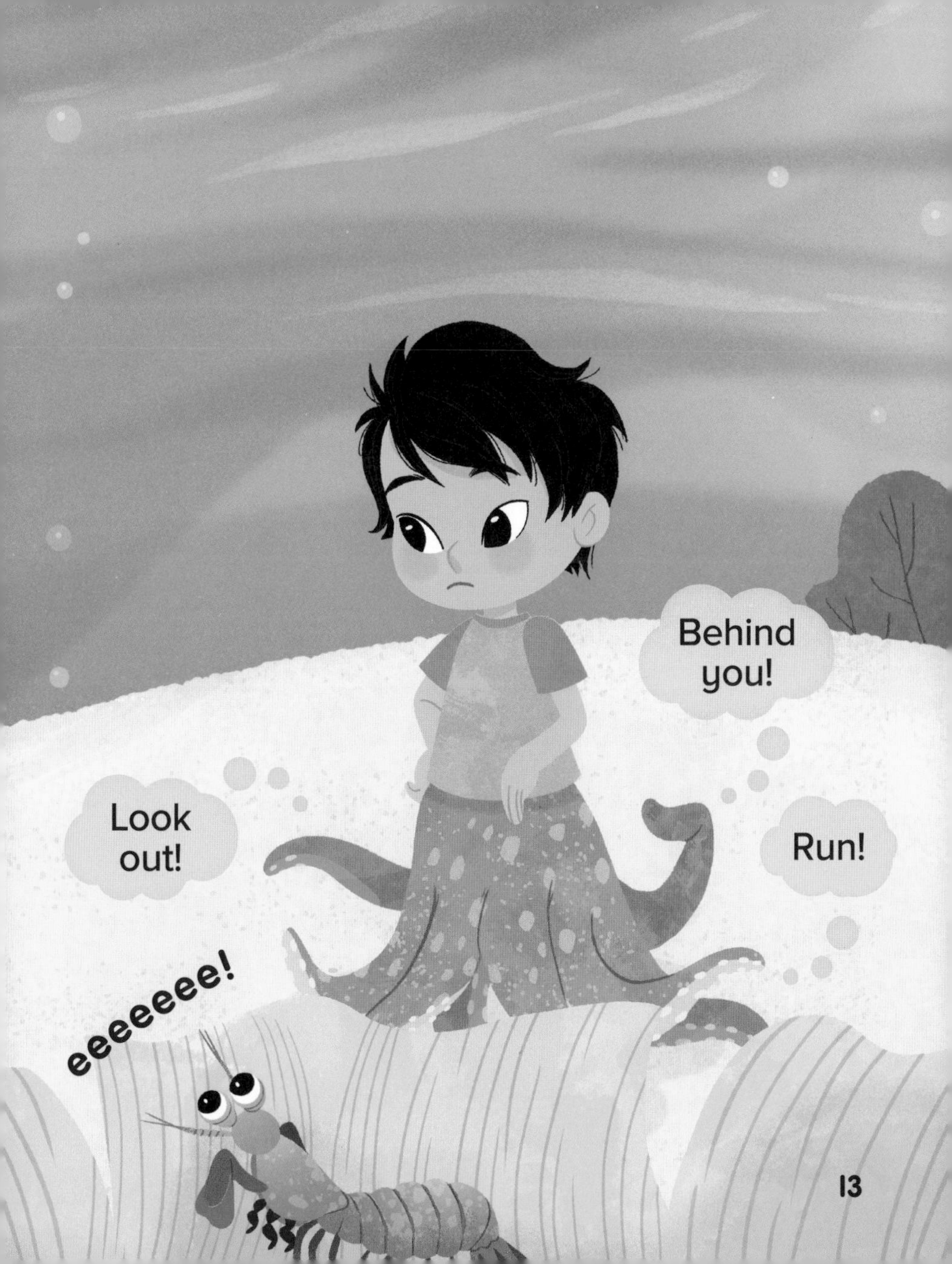
Behind you!
Look out!
Run!
eeeeeee!

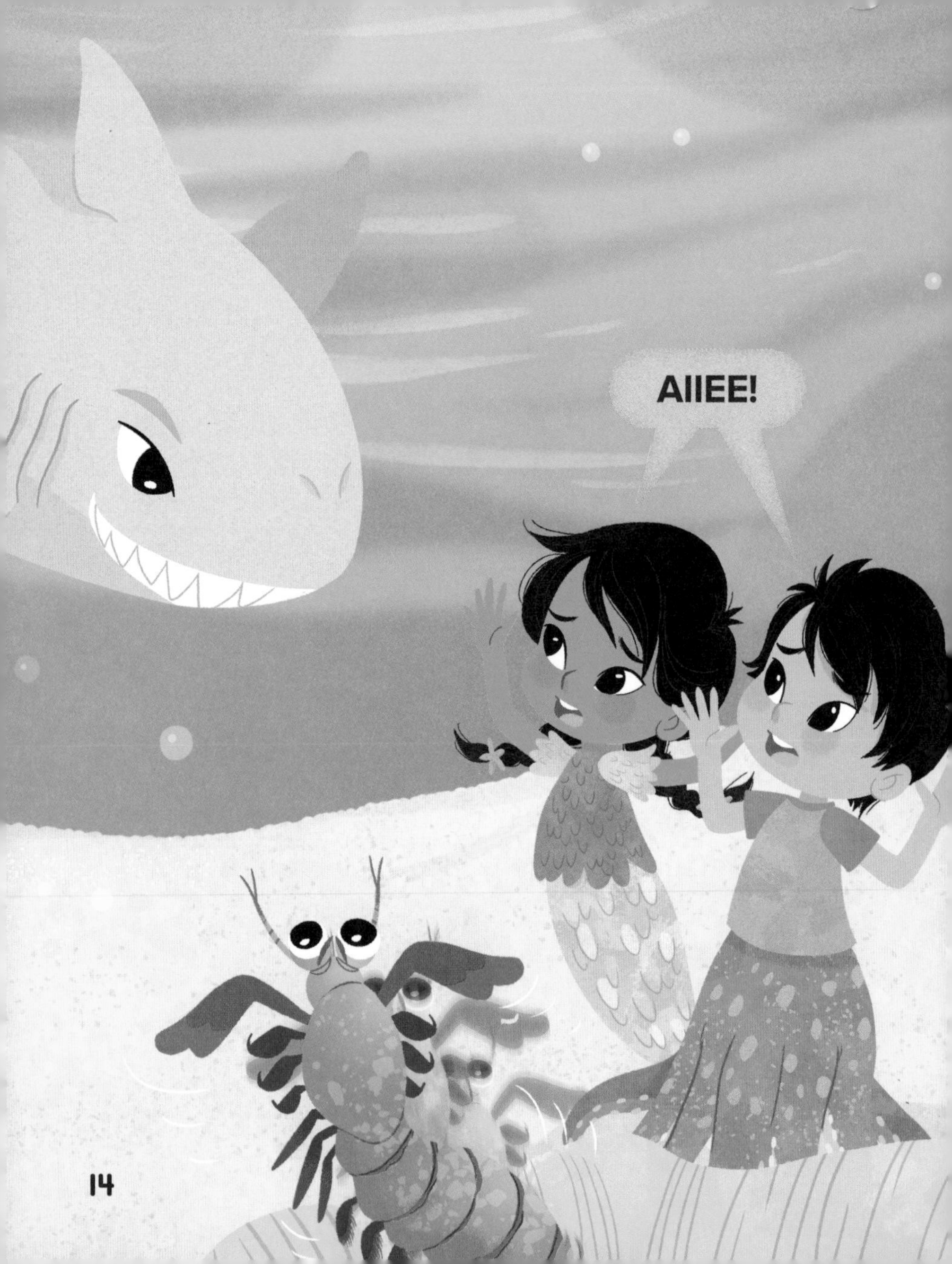
AIIEE!

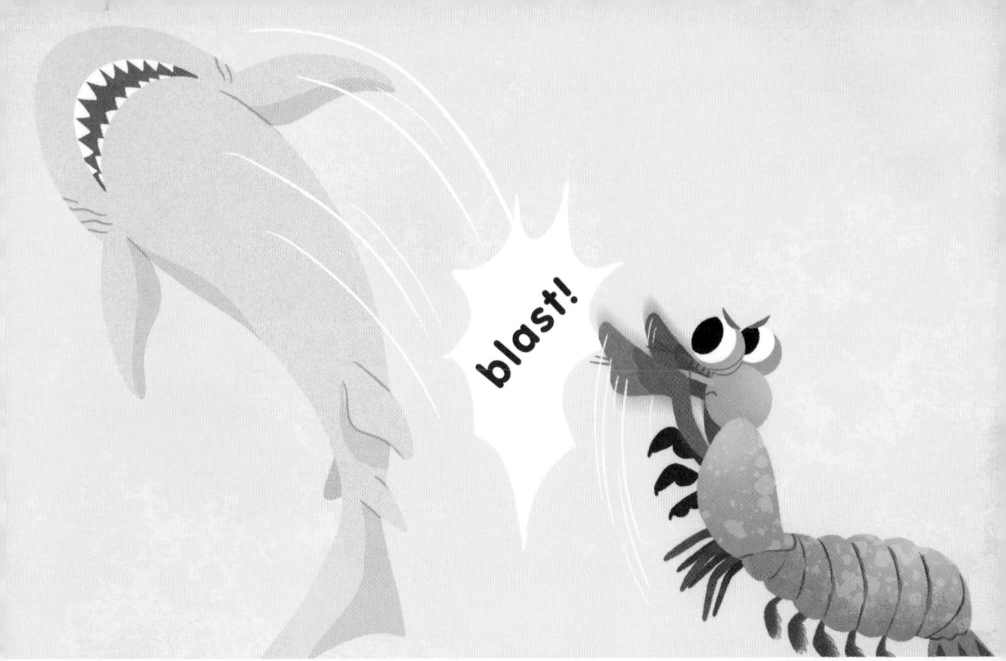
blast!

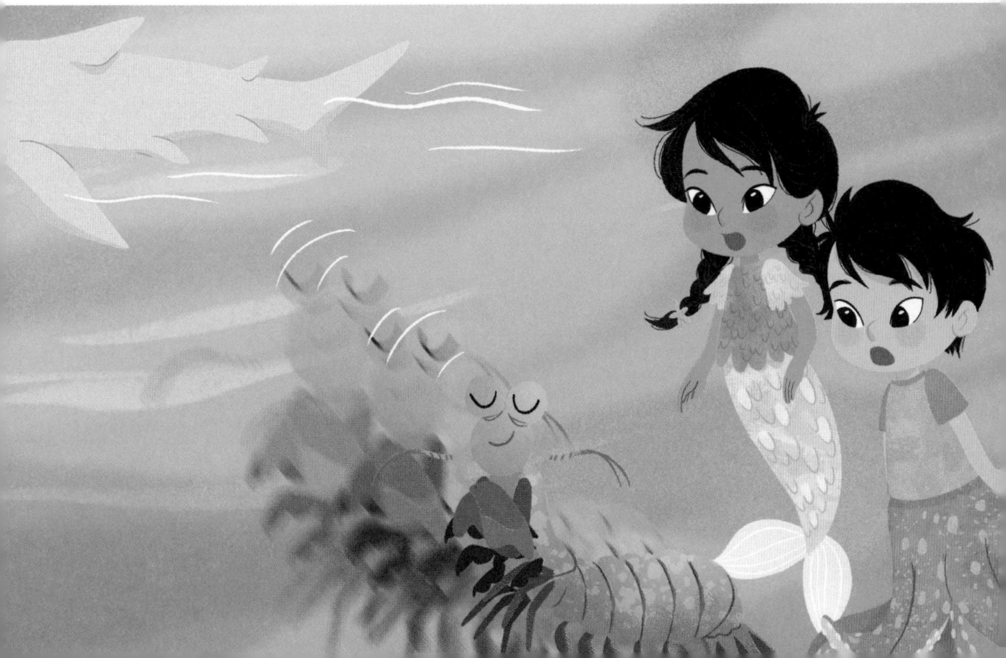

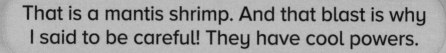

That is a mantis shrimp. And that blast is why I said to be careful! They have cool powers.

Wow! Thanks for saving us from that shark.

I guess this tiny shrimp broke all those things in town.

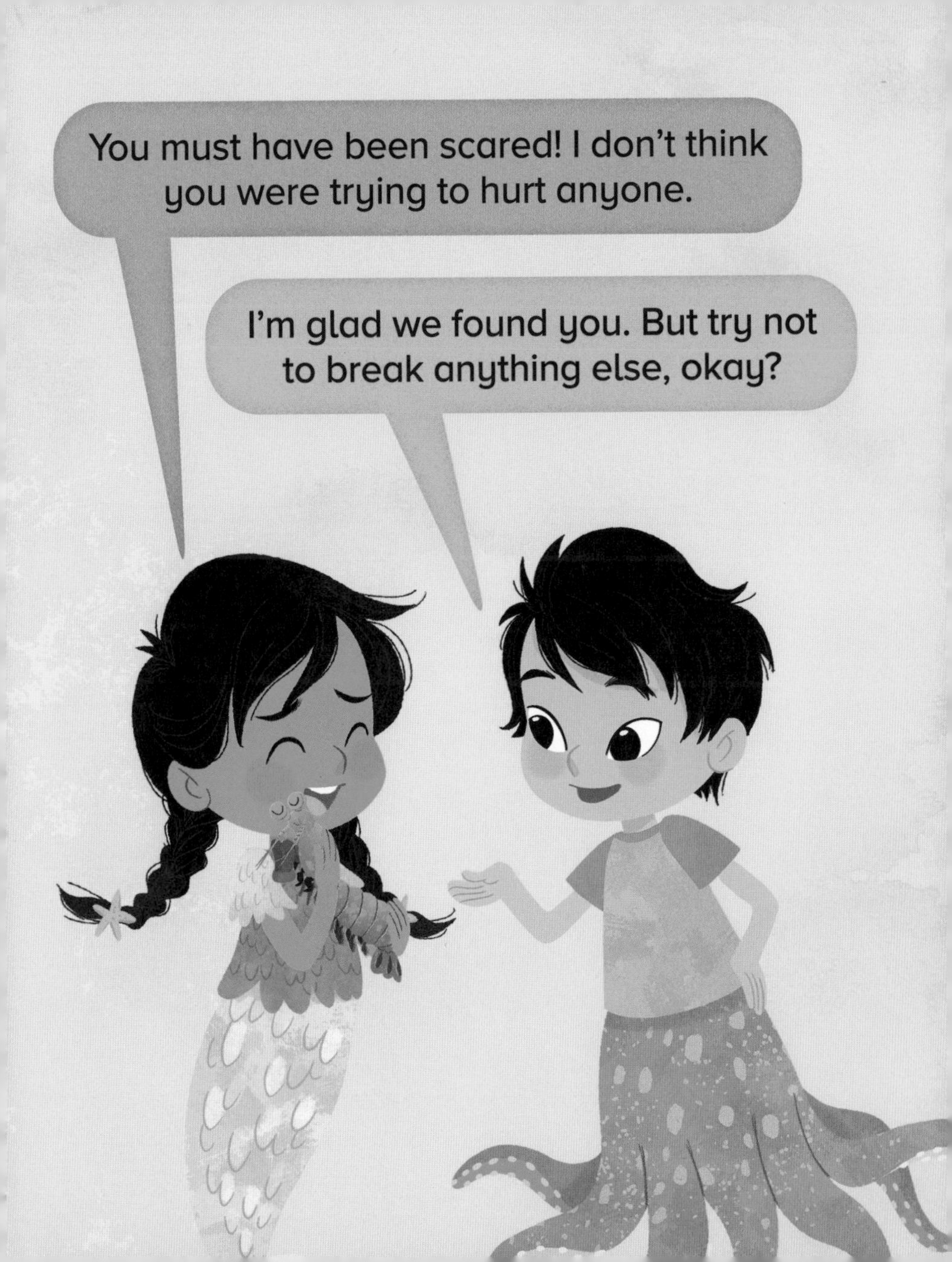
You must have been scared! I don't think you were trying to hurt anyone.
I'm glad we found you. But try not to break anything else, okay?

DID YOU KNOW?

Mantis shrimp are very small. But they can make themselves look much bigger.

They are also very strong! They punch water to create shock waves. Some shock waves are strong enough to break glass.

LIBRARIAN

It is a bad idea to get into a fight with a mantis shrimp!

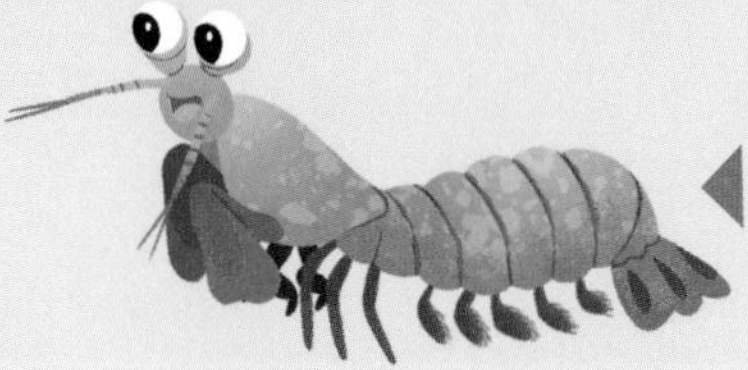

Mantis shrimp usually grow to be about four inches long.

Mantis shrimp can make themselves look really big.

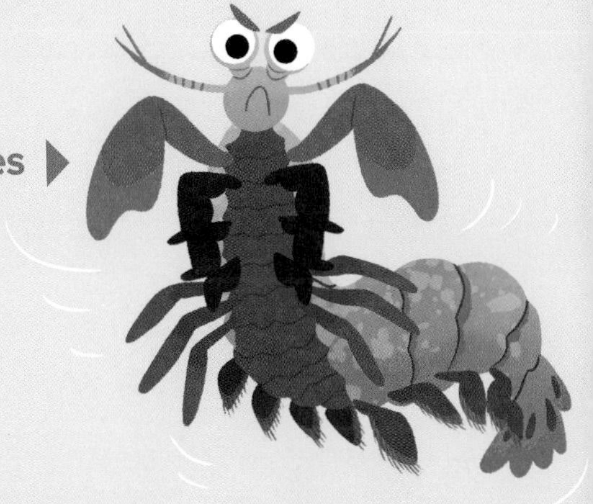

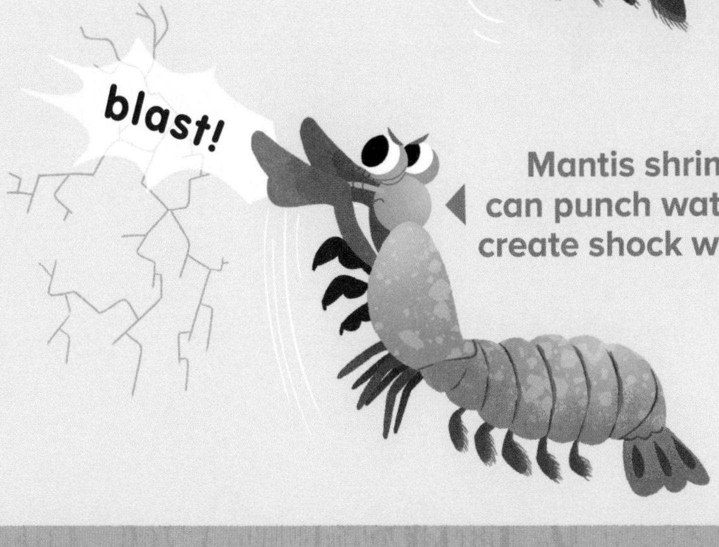
blast!

Mantis shrimp can punch water to create shock waves!

FINDING FAMILY

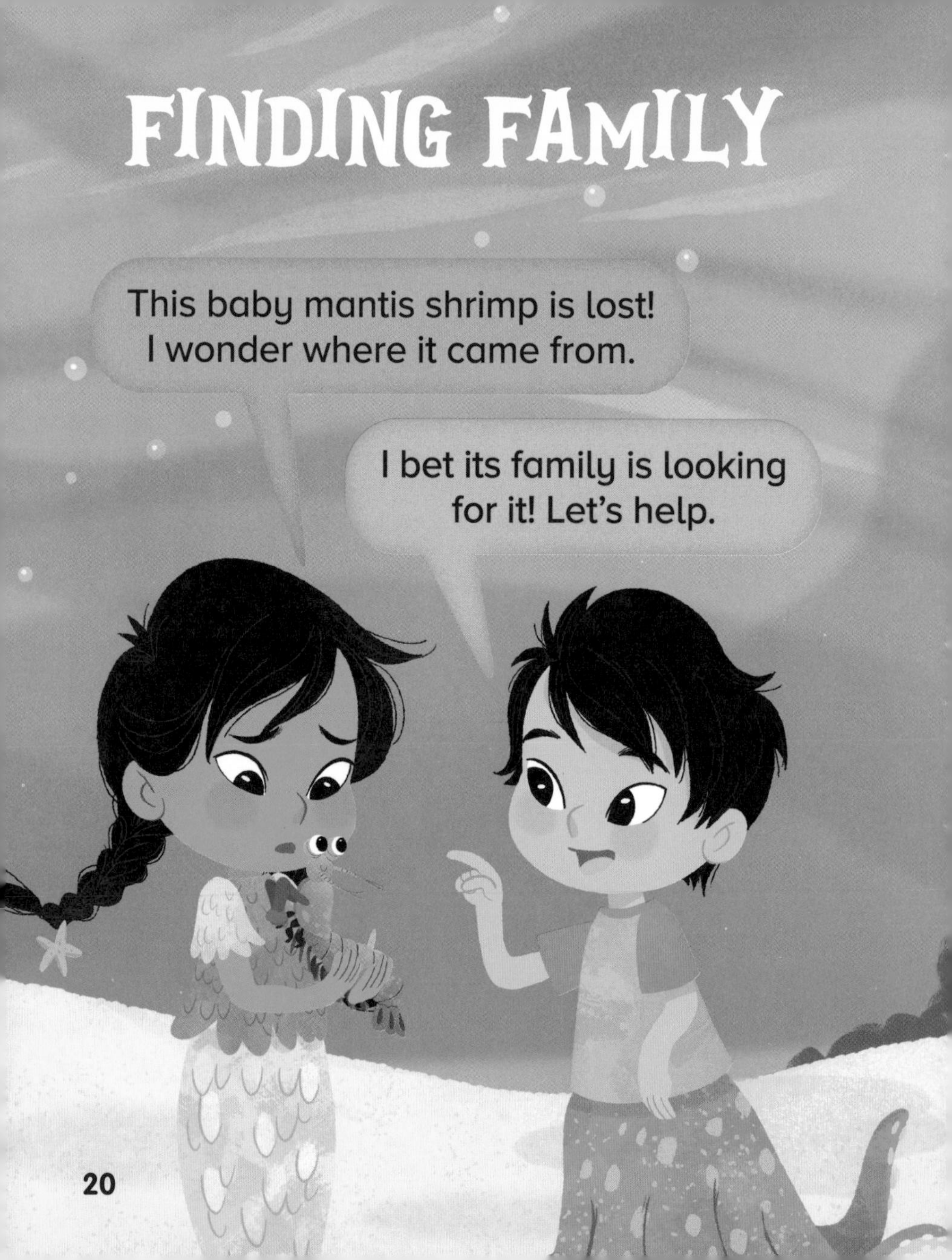
This baby mantis shrimp is lost! I wonder where it came from.
I bet its family is looking for it! Let's help.

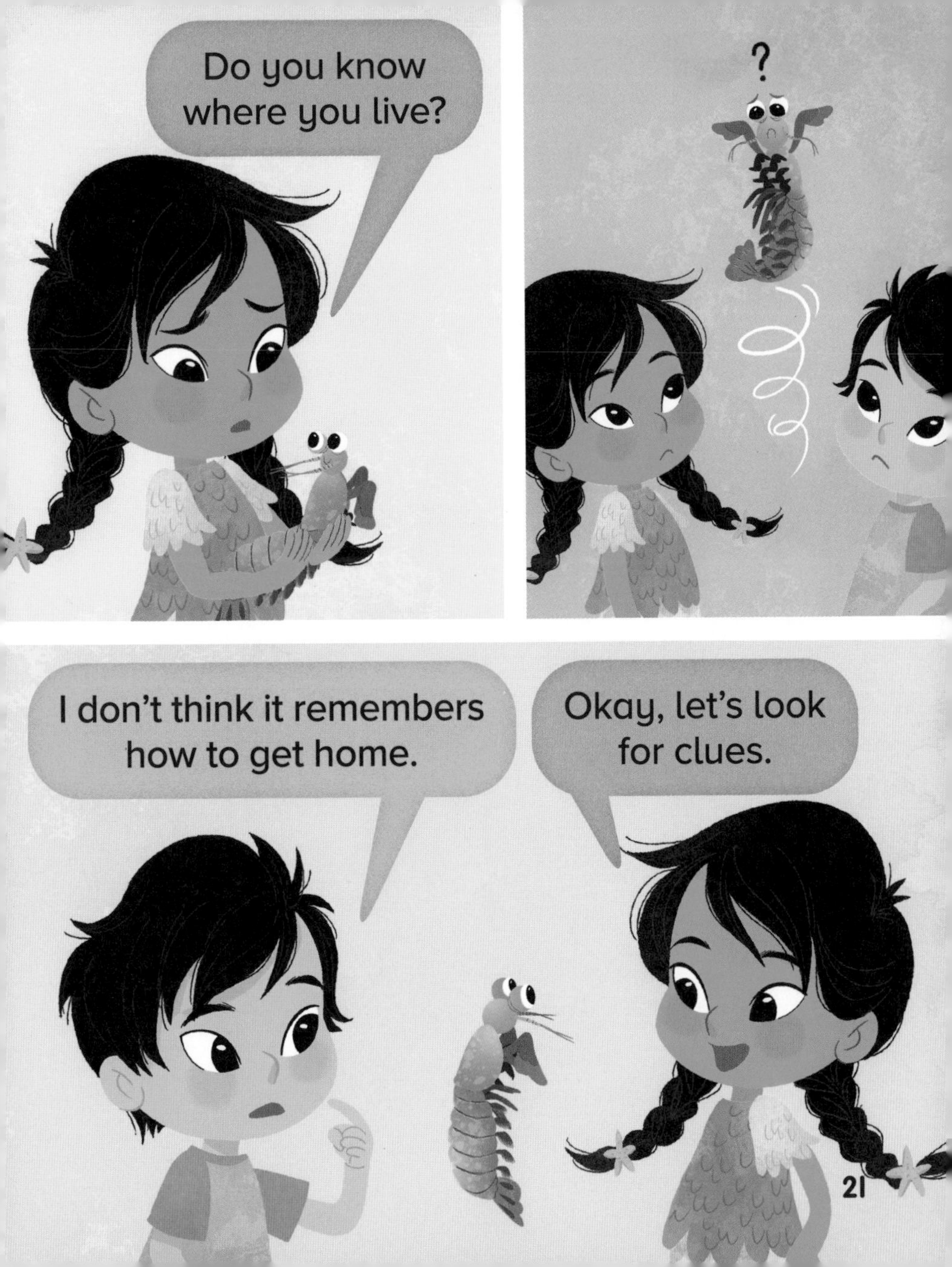
Do you know where you live?
?
I don't think it remembers how to get home.
Okay, let's look for clues.

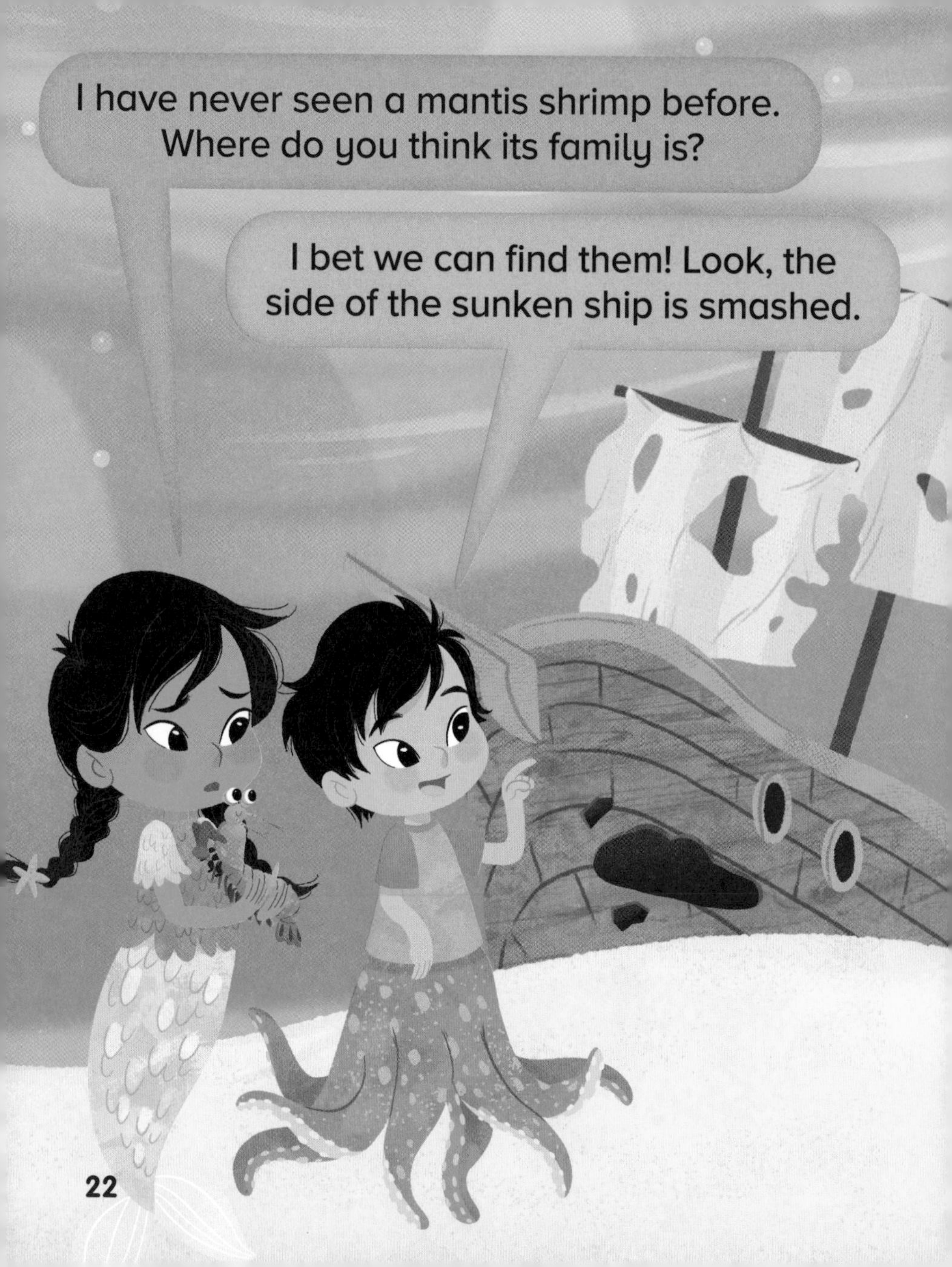
I have never seen a mantis shrimp before. Where do you think its family is?
I bet we can find them! Look, the side of the sunken ship is smashed.

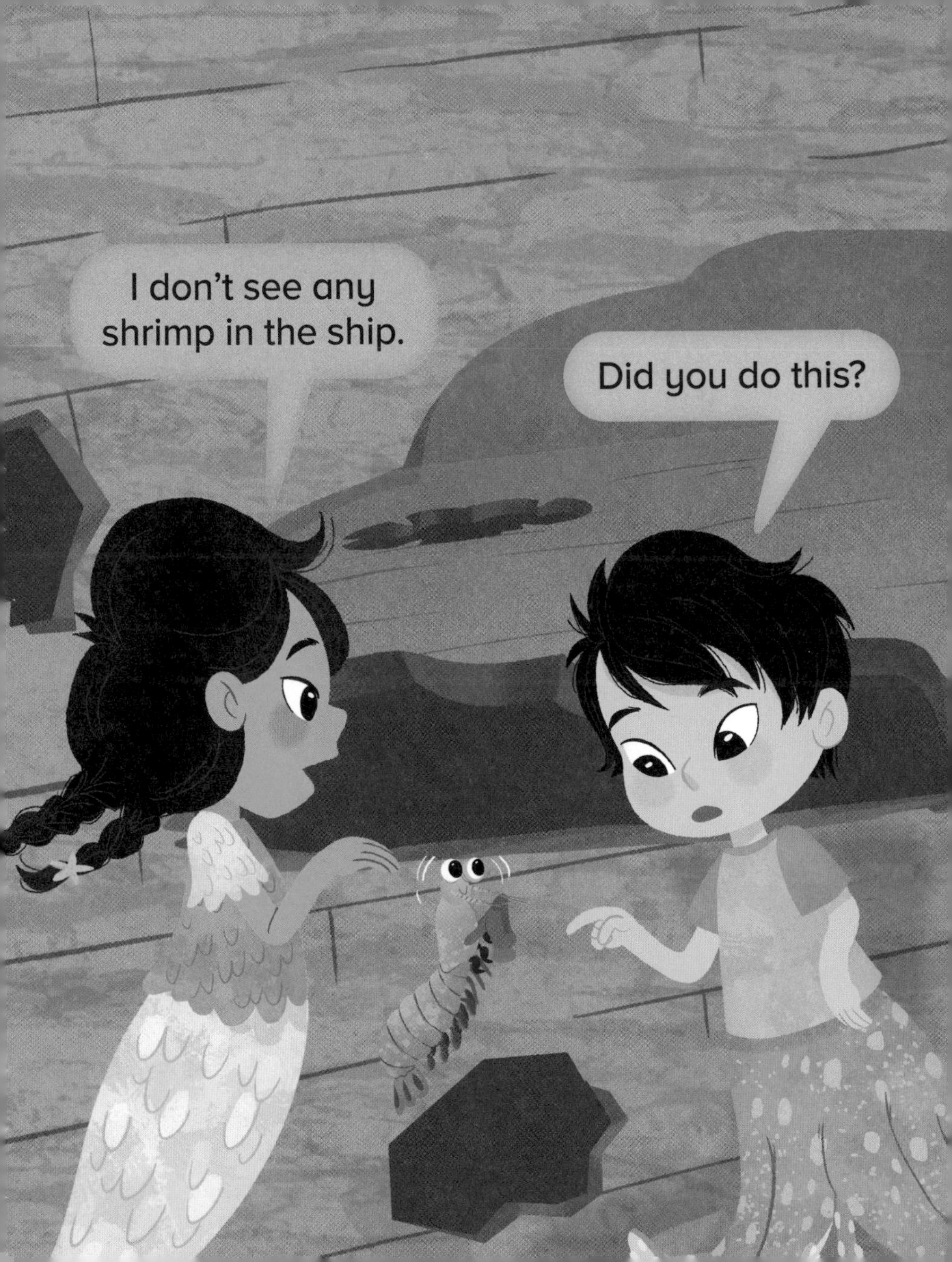
I don't see any shrimp in the ship.
Did you do this?

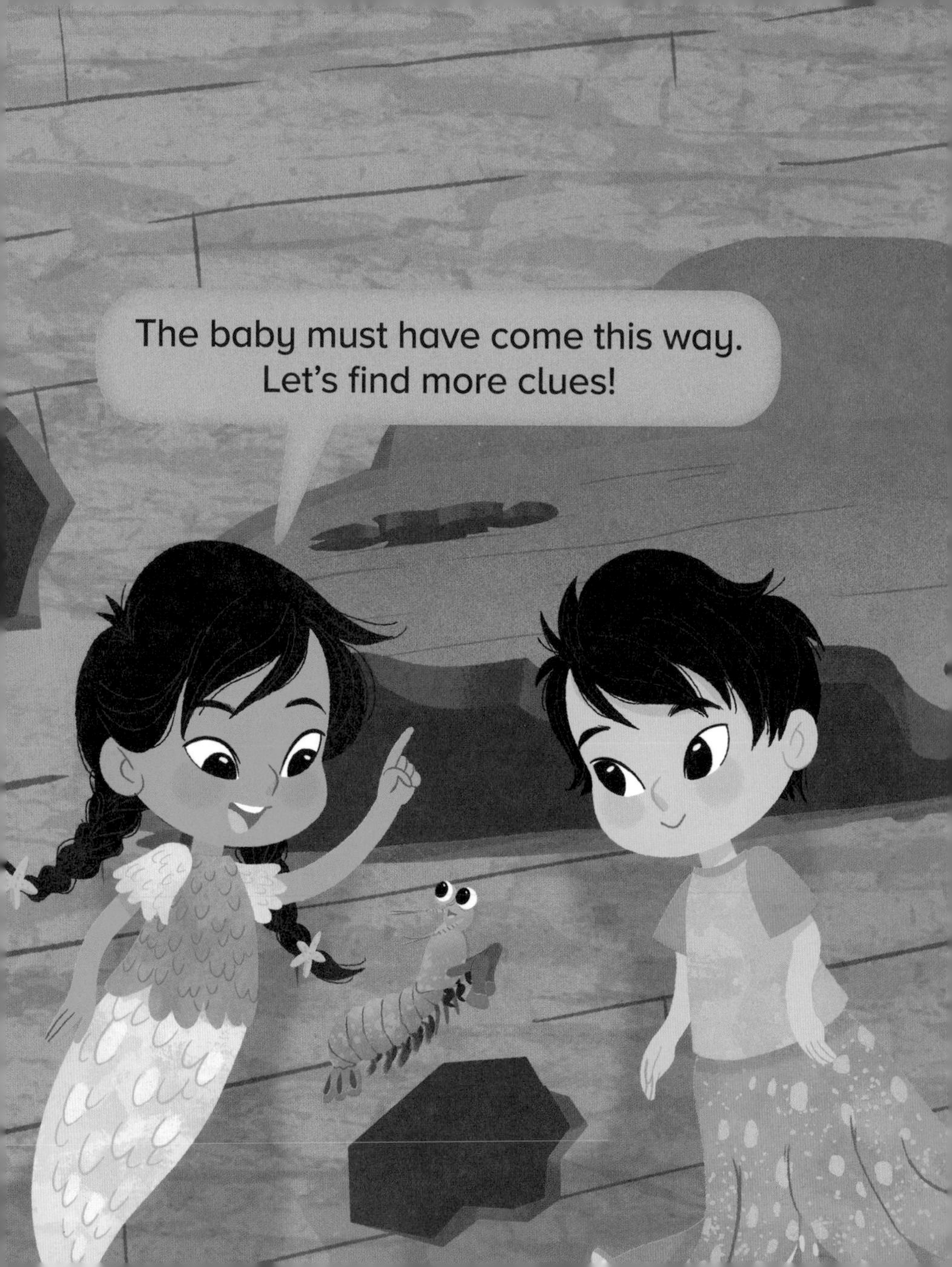
The baby must have come this way. Let's find more clues!

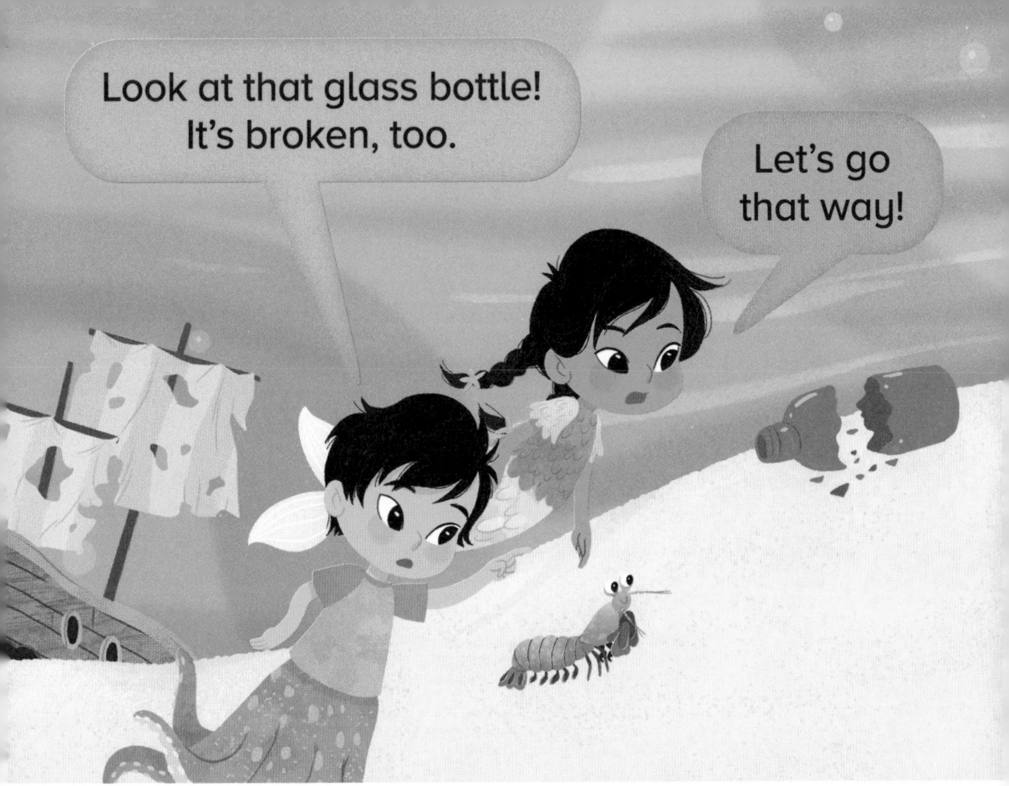
Look at that glass bottle! It's broken, too.
Let's go that way!

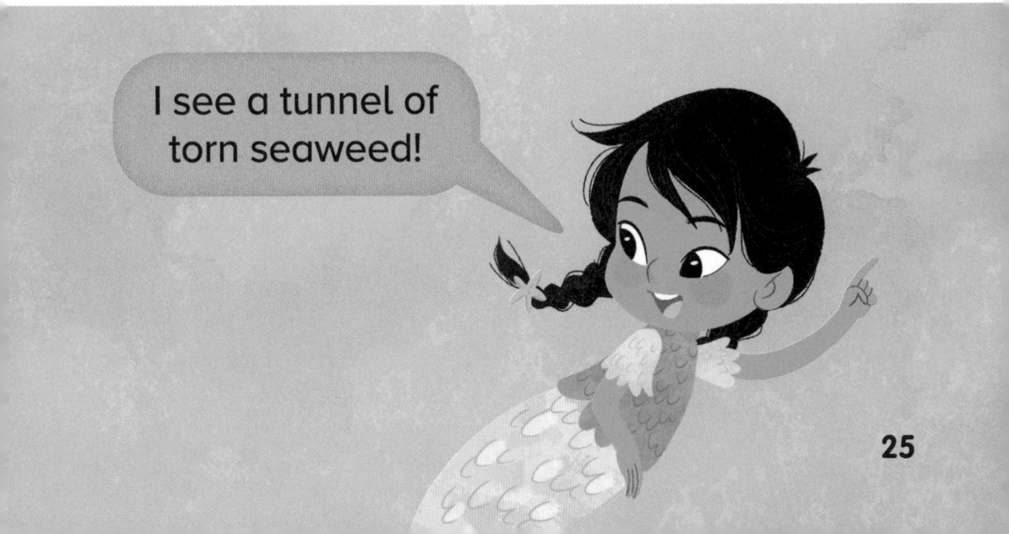
I see a tunnel of torn seaweed!

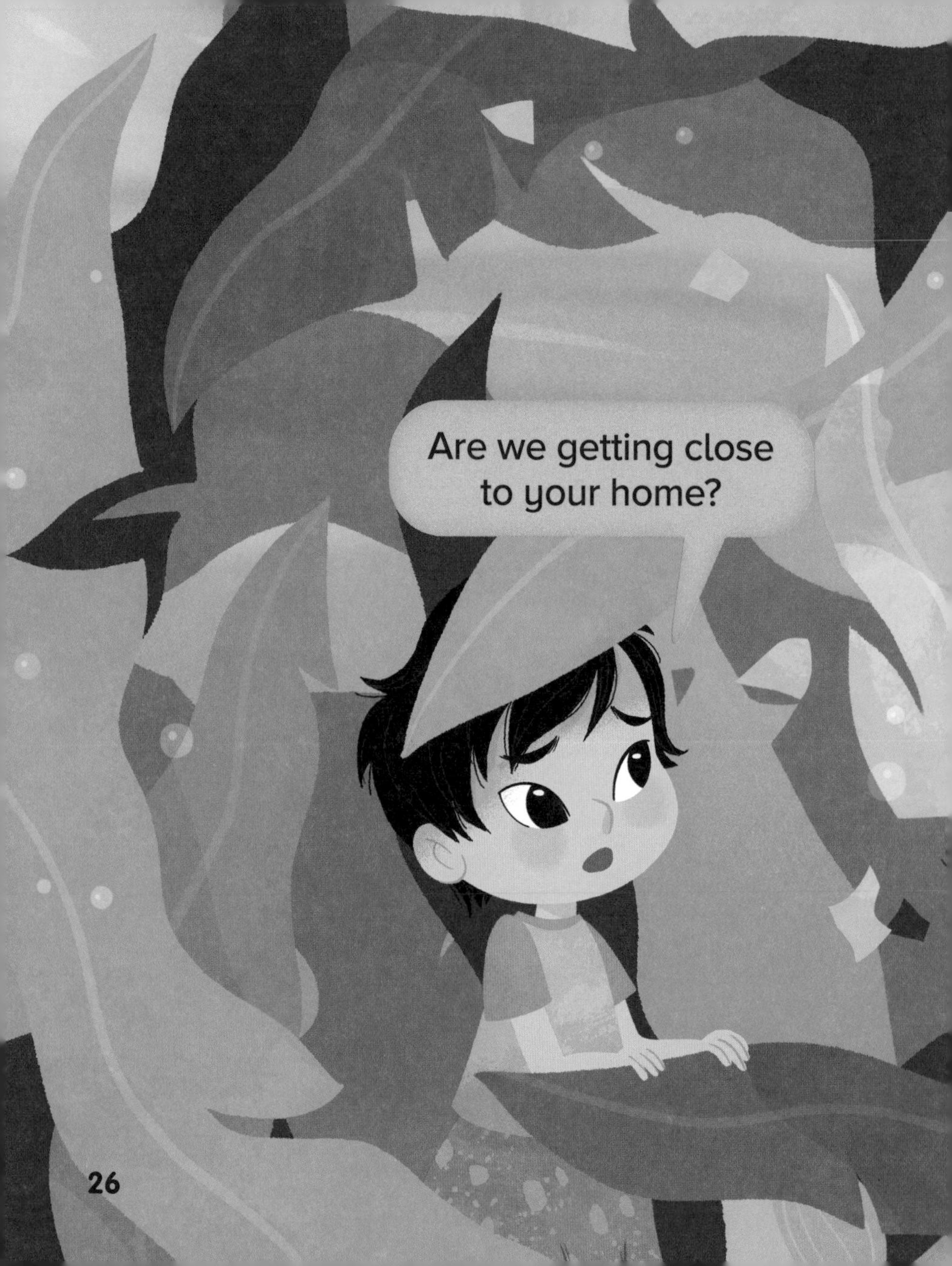
Are we getting close to your home?

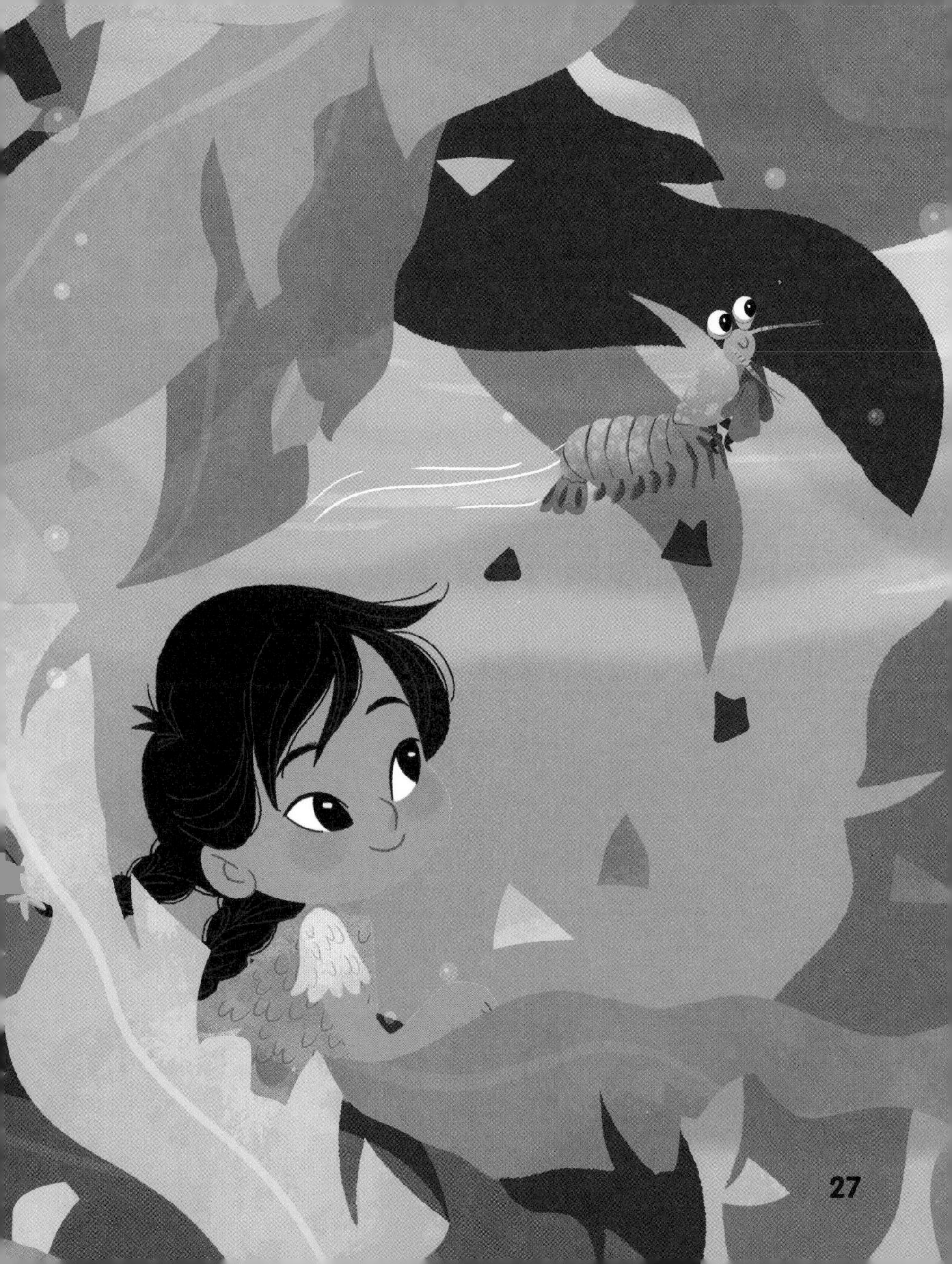

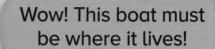

Wow! This boat must be where it lives!

I want to explore.

So many holes!

I wish we could make holes.

28

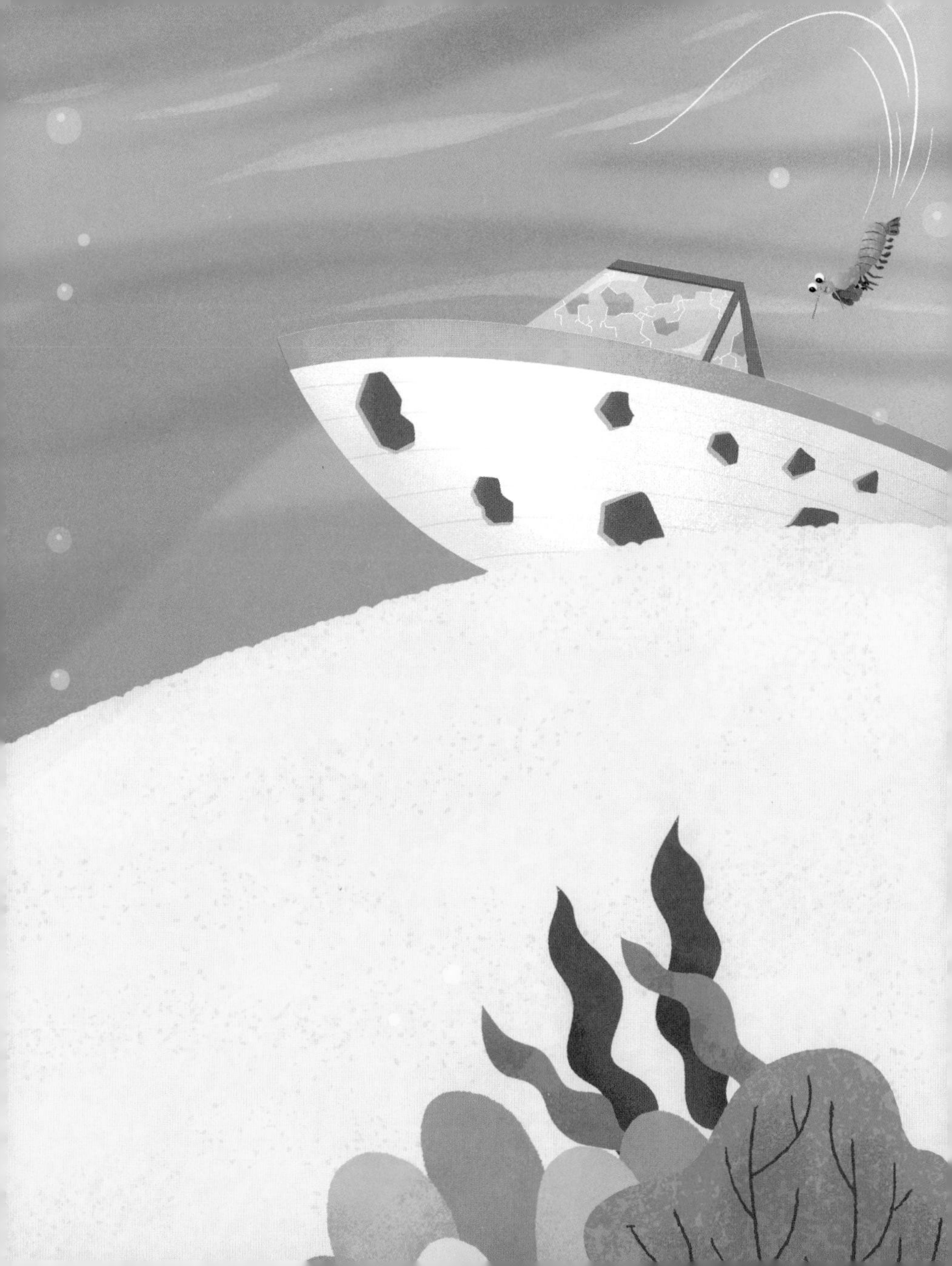

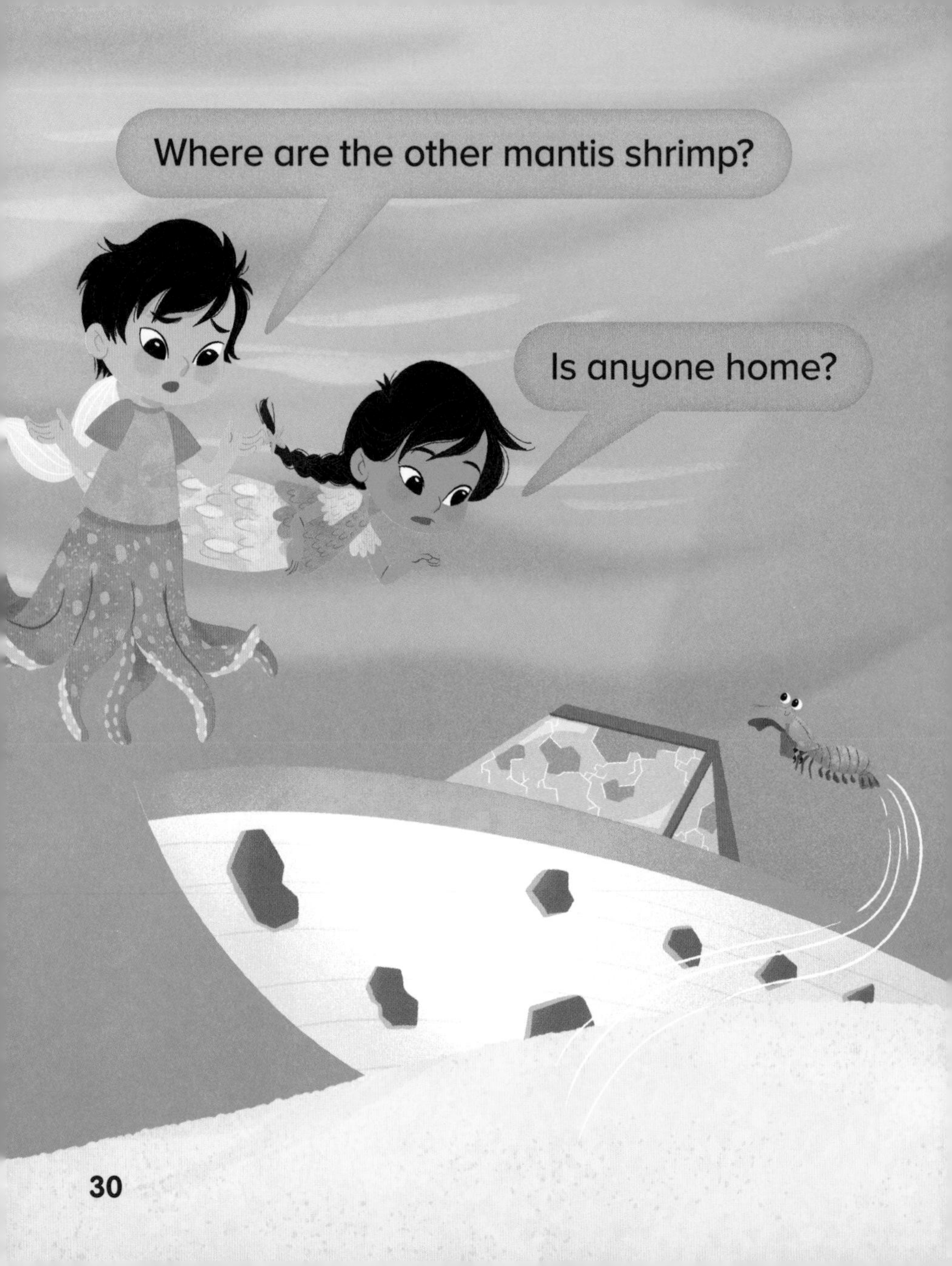
Where are the other mantis shrimp?
Is anyone home?

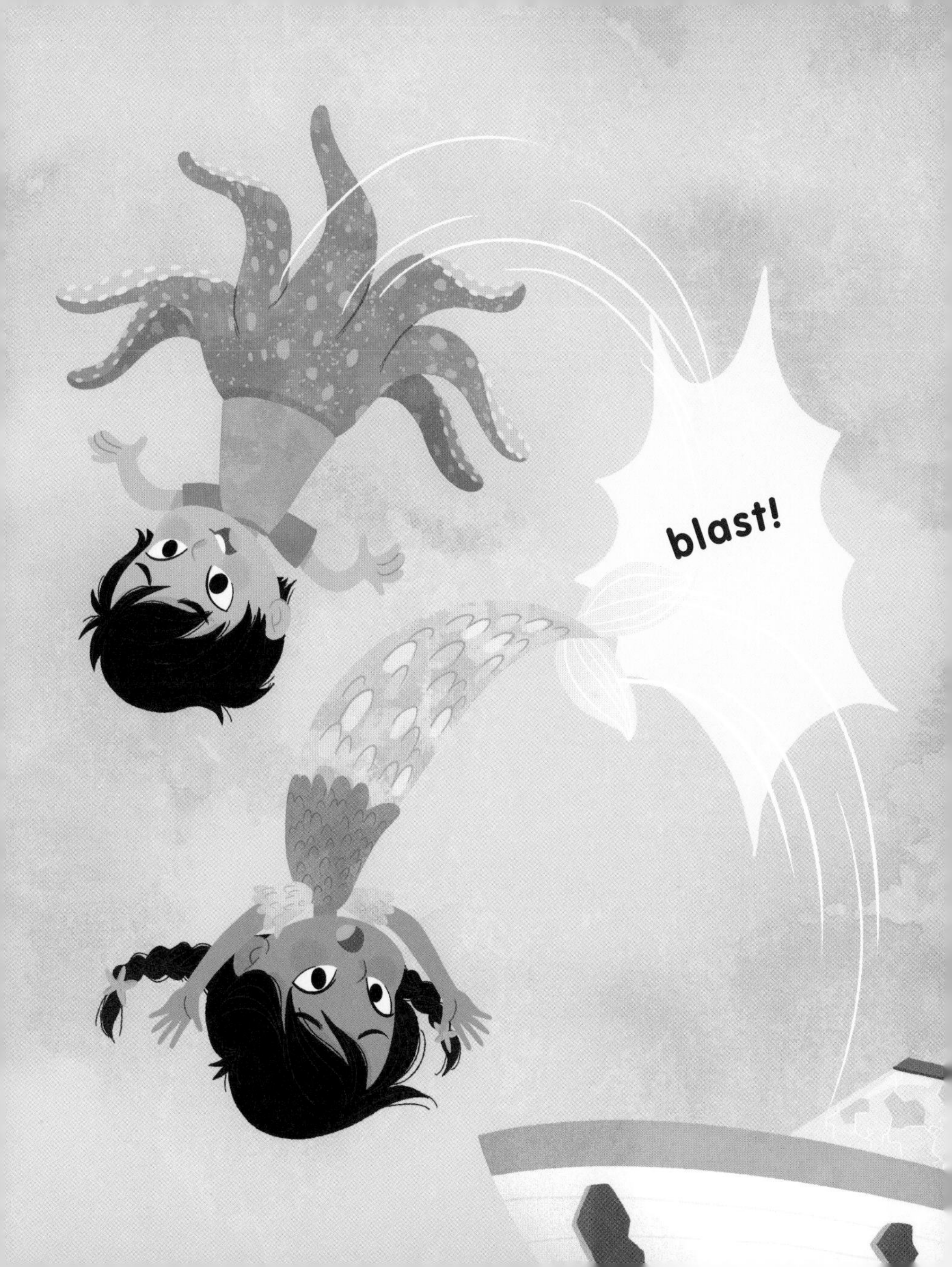
blast!

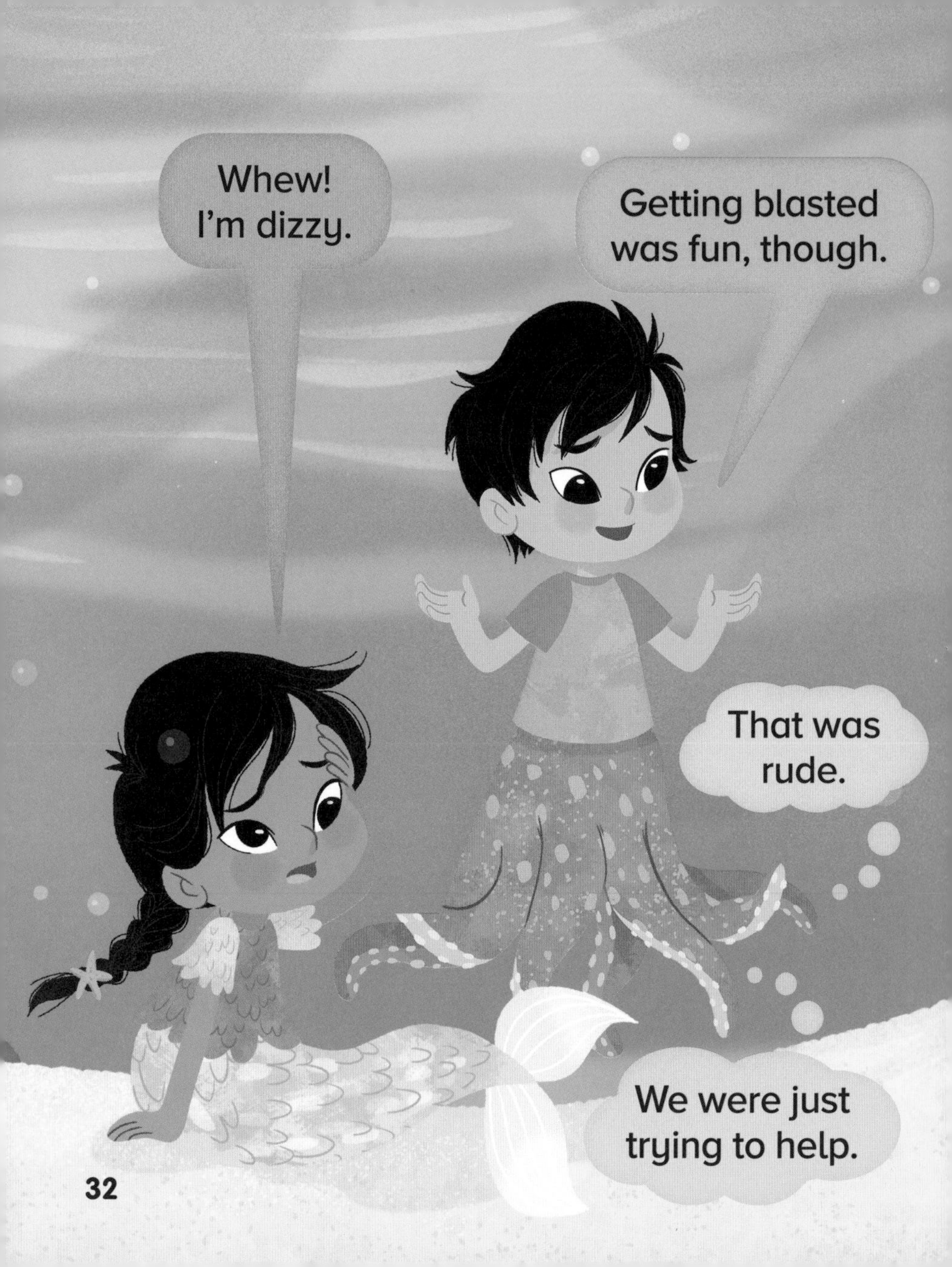
Whew! I'm dizzy.
Getting blasted was fun, though.
That was rude.
We were just trying to help.

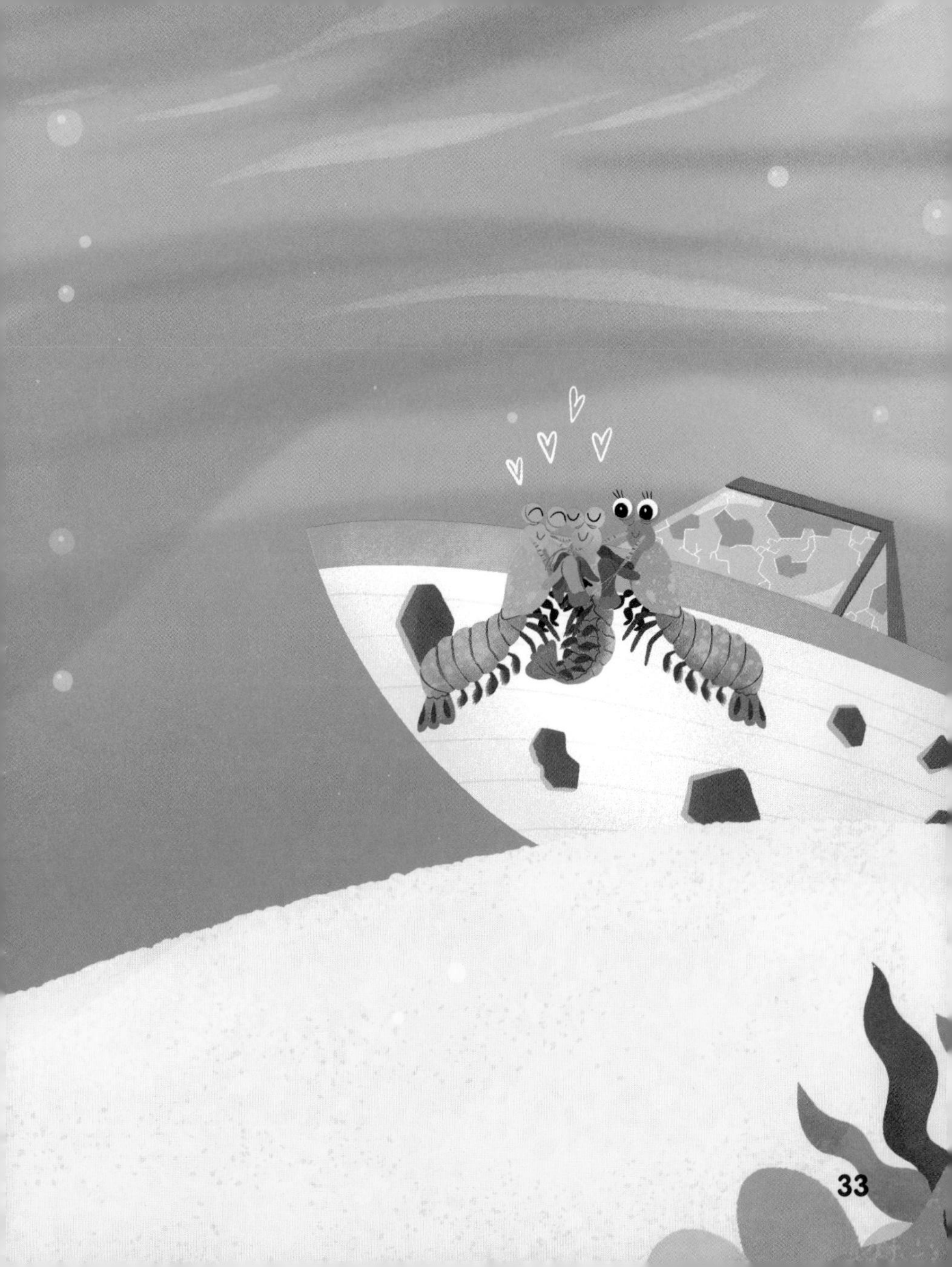

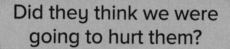

Did they think we were going to hurt them?

Probably! We are much bigger than they are.

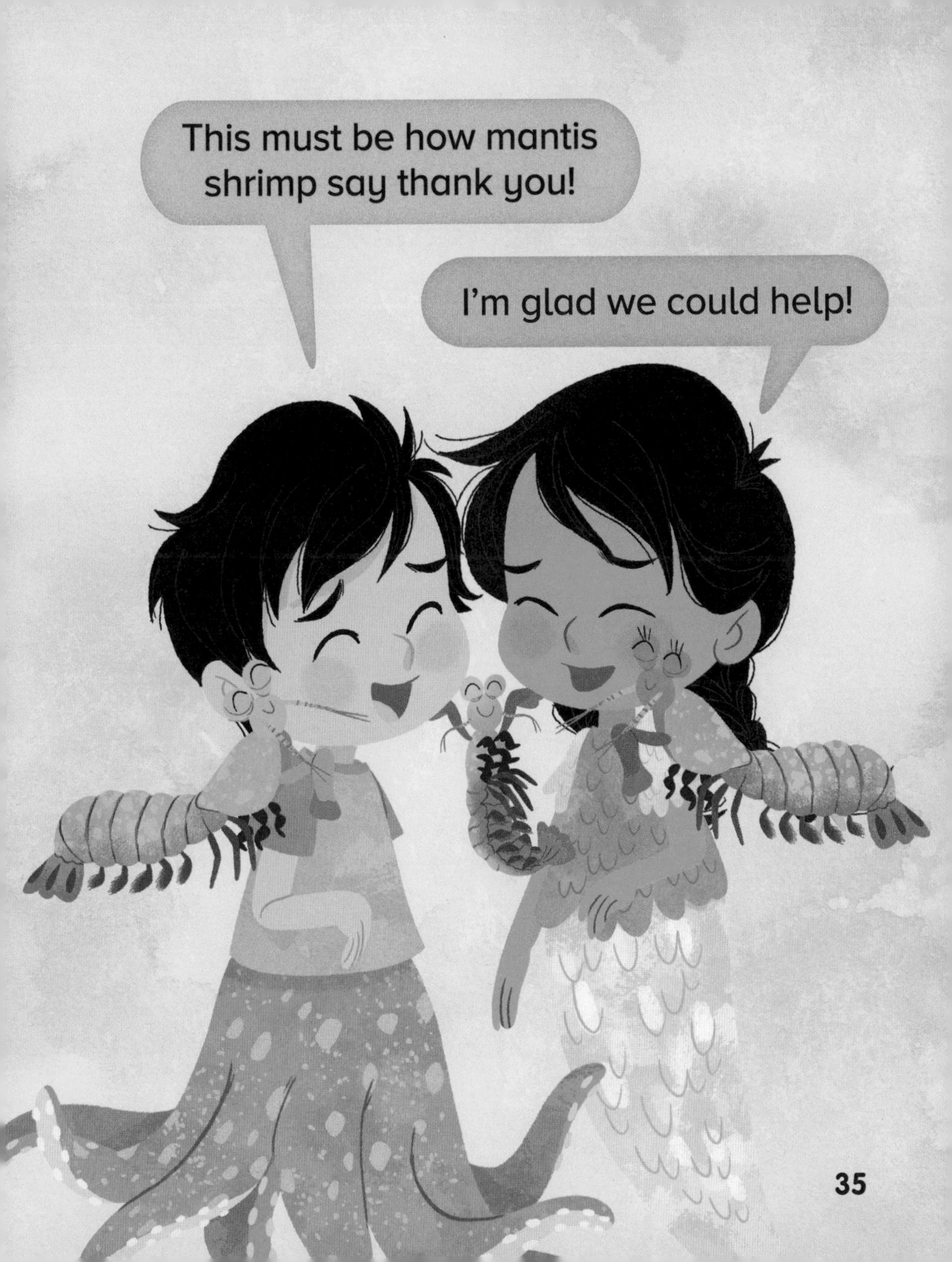
This must be how mantis shrimp say thank you!
I'm glad we could help!

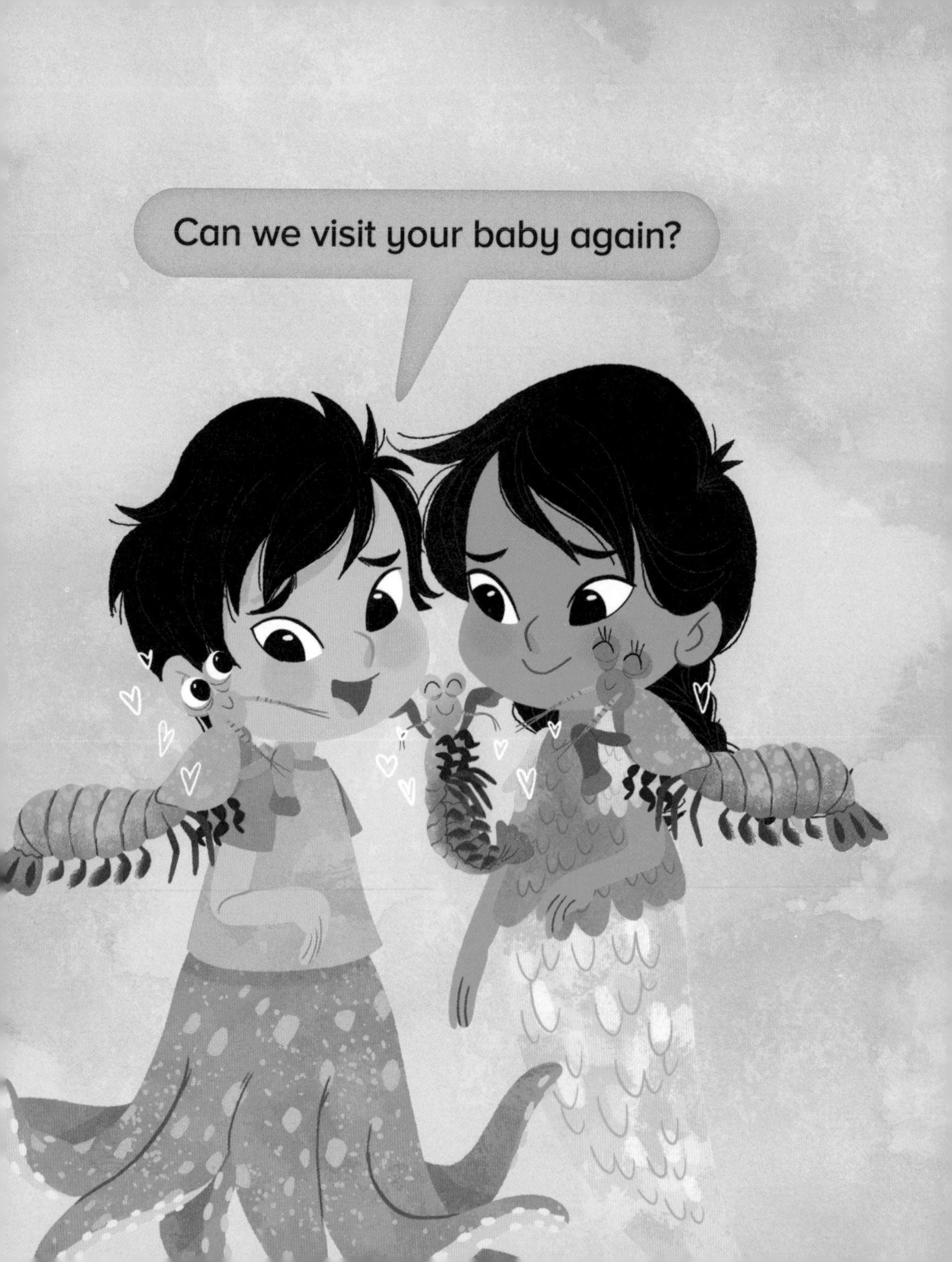
Can we visit your baby again?

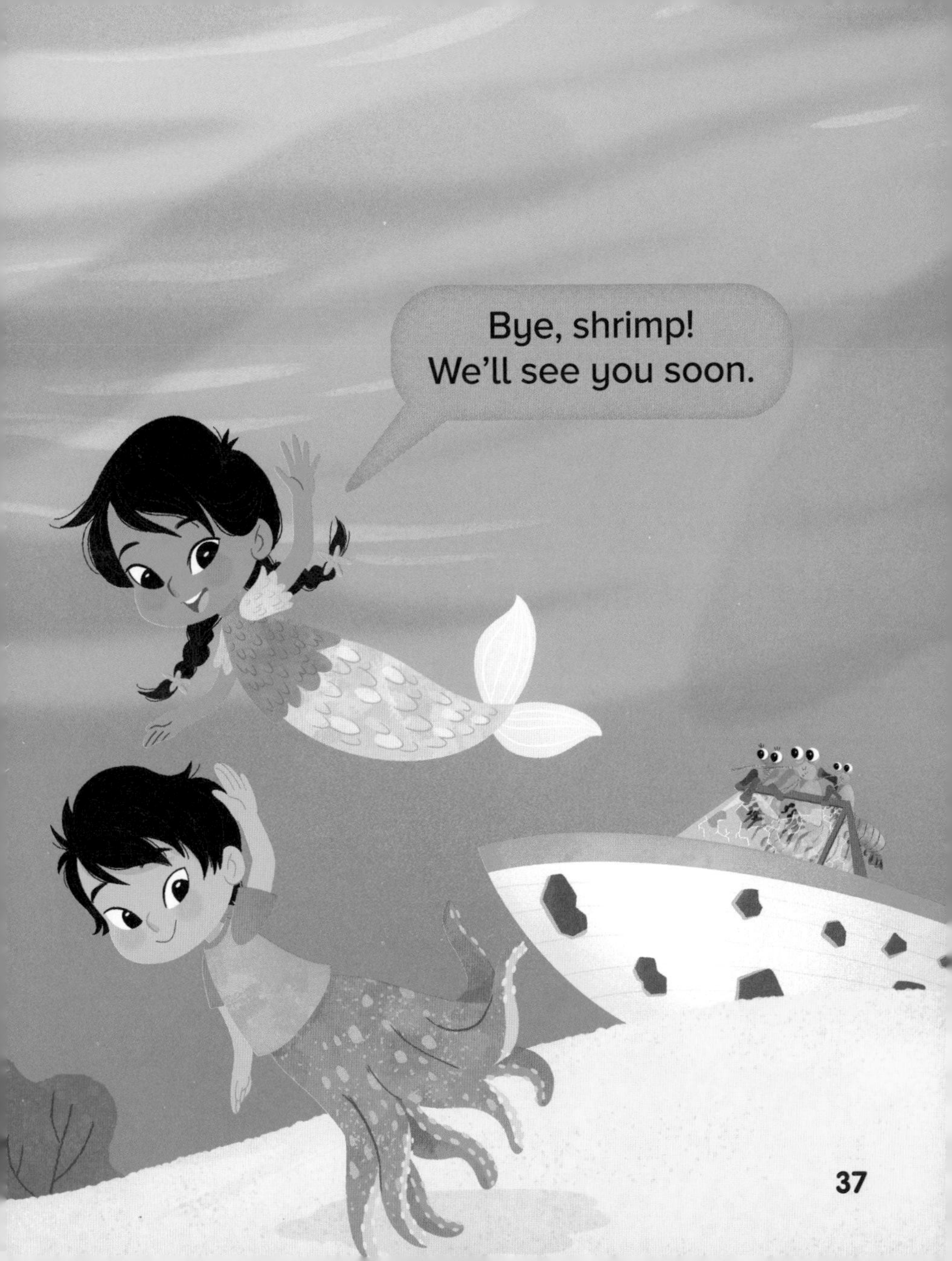
Bye, shrimp!
We'll see you soon.

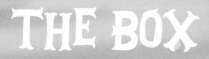

THE BOX

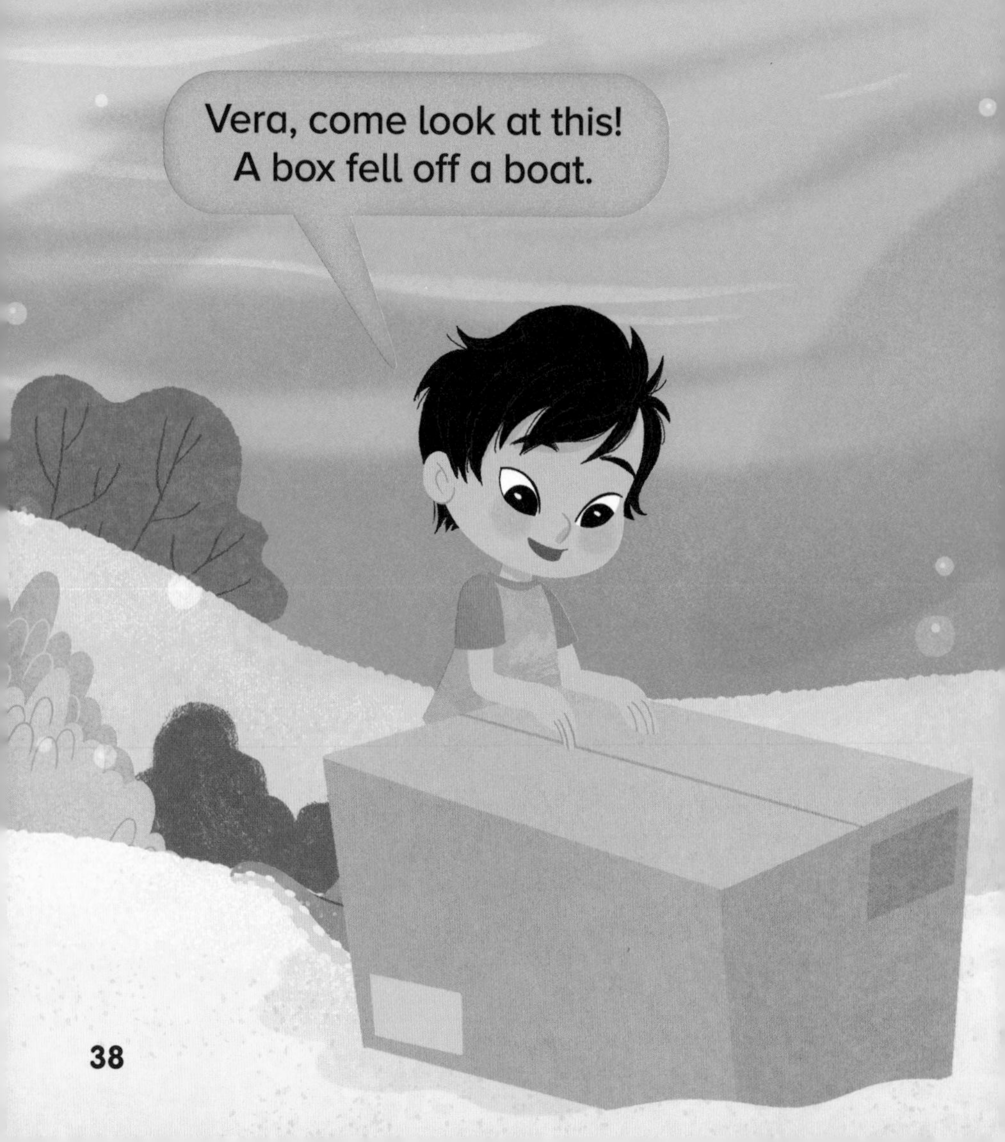
Vera, come look at this!
A box fell off a boat.

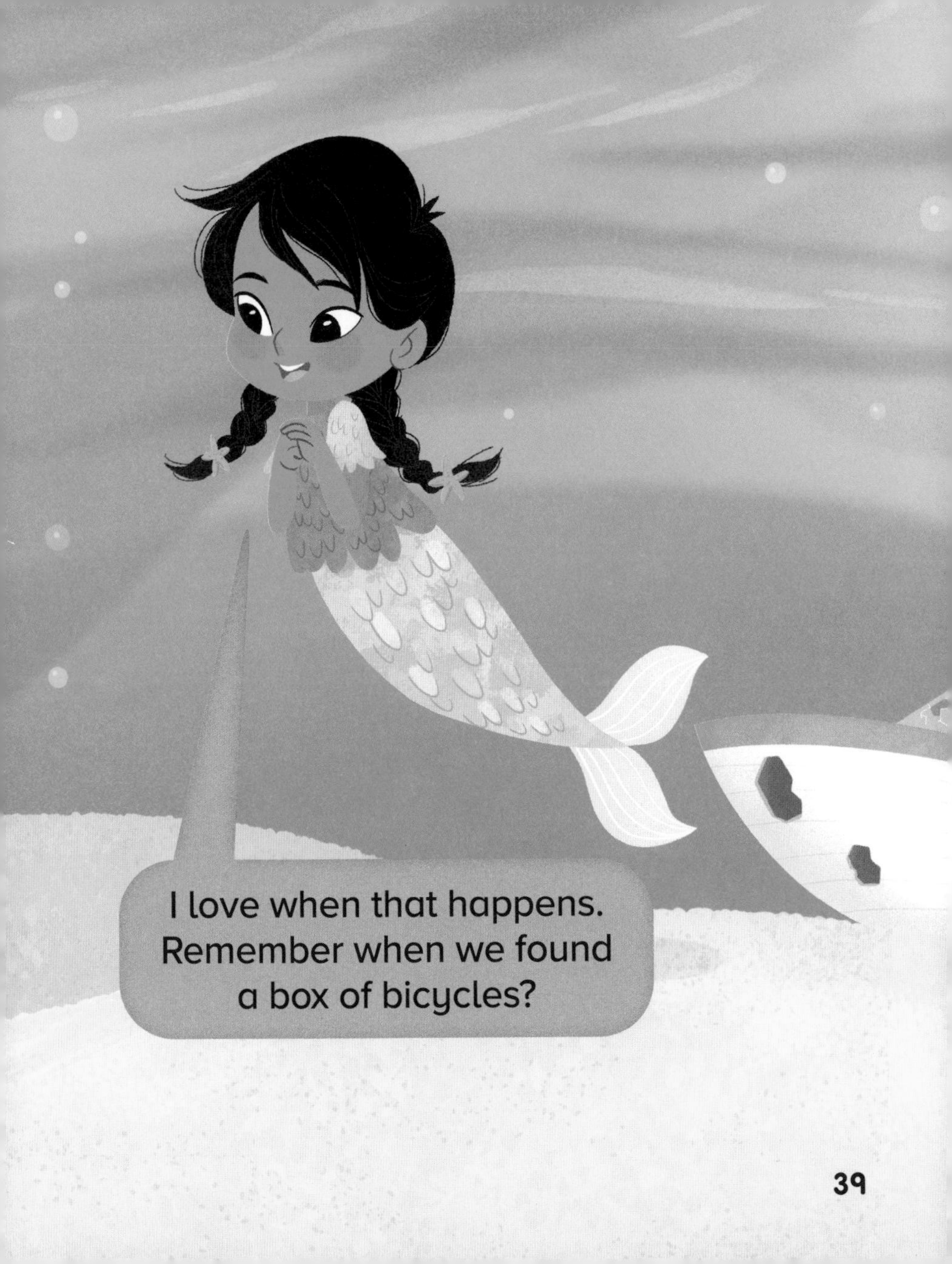
I love when that happens.
Remember when we found
a box of bicycles?

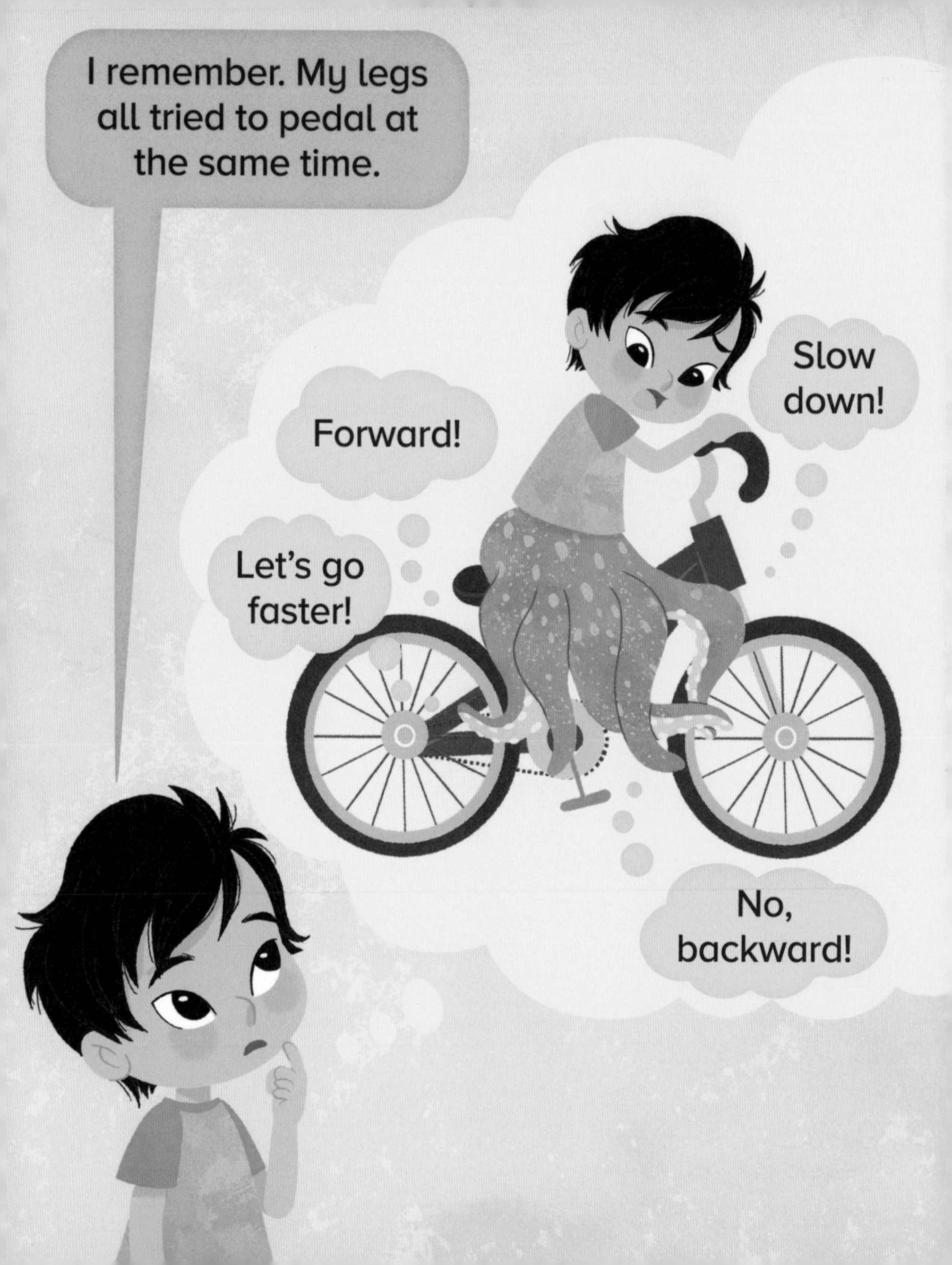
I remember. My legs all tried to pedal at the same time.
Forward!
Slow down!
Let's go faster!
No, backward!

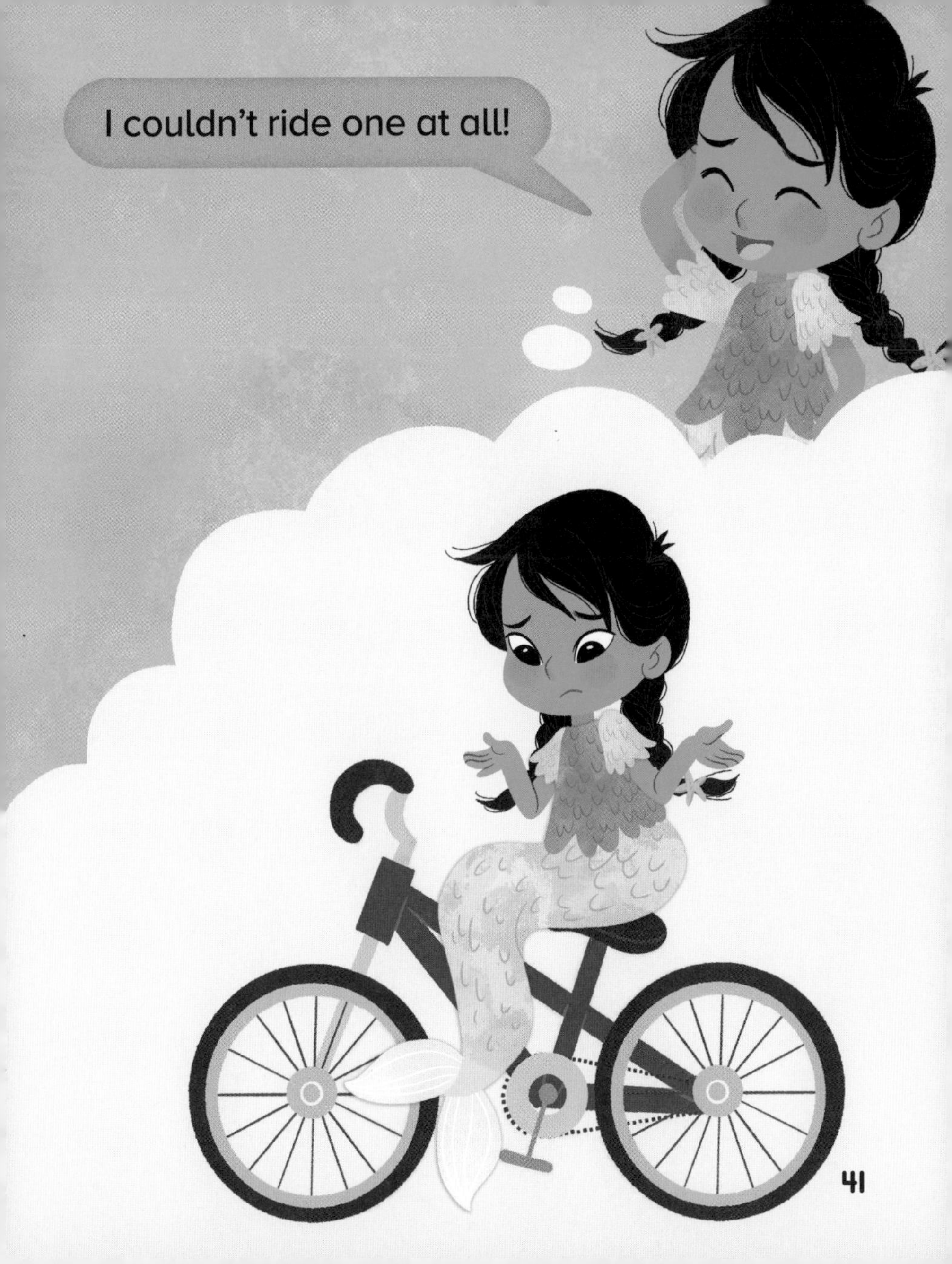
I couldn't ride one at all!

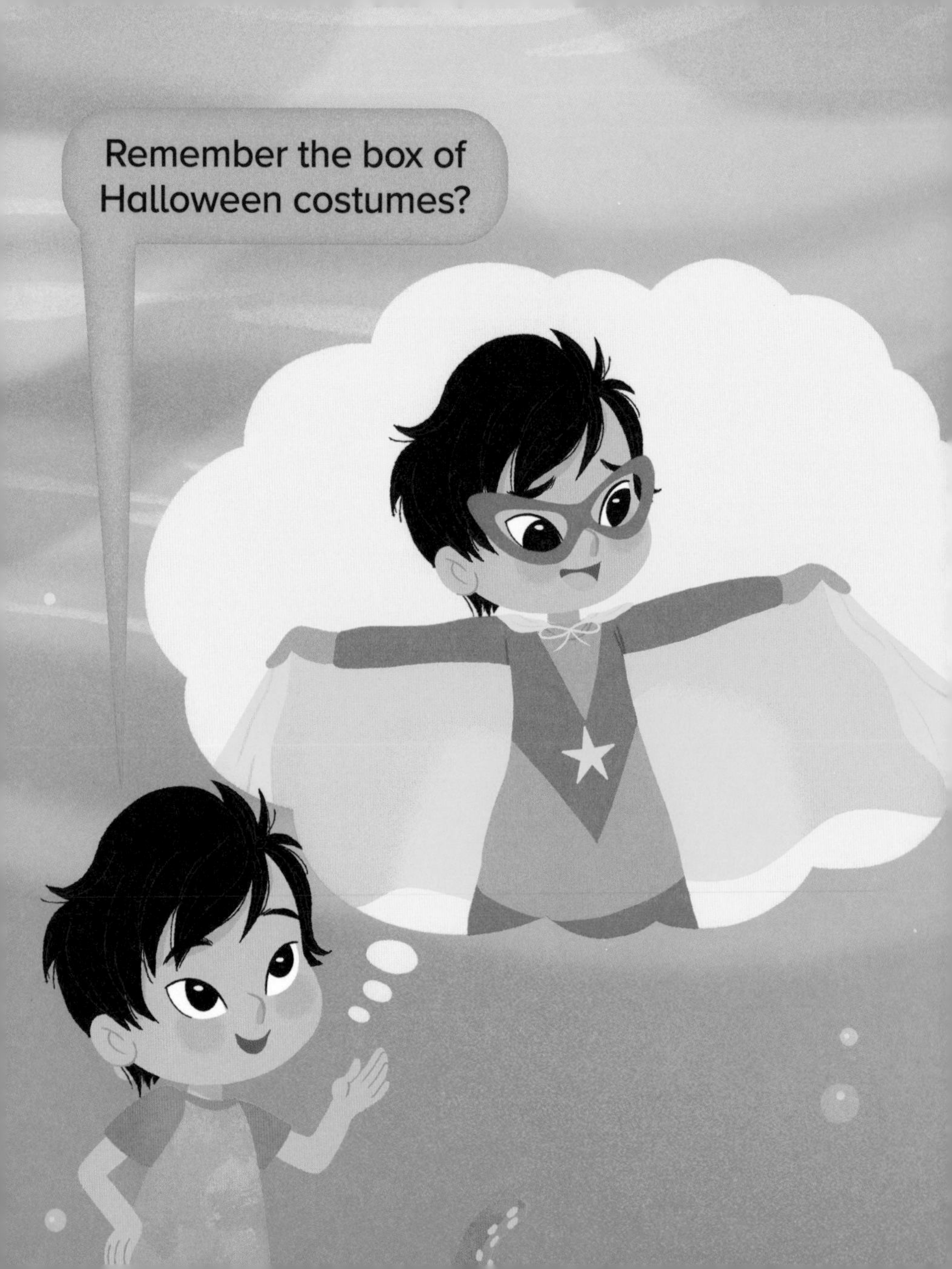
Remember the box of Halloween costumes?

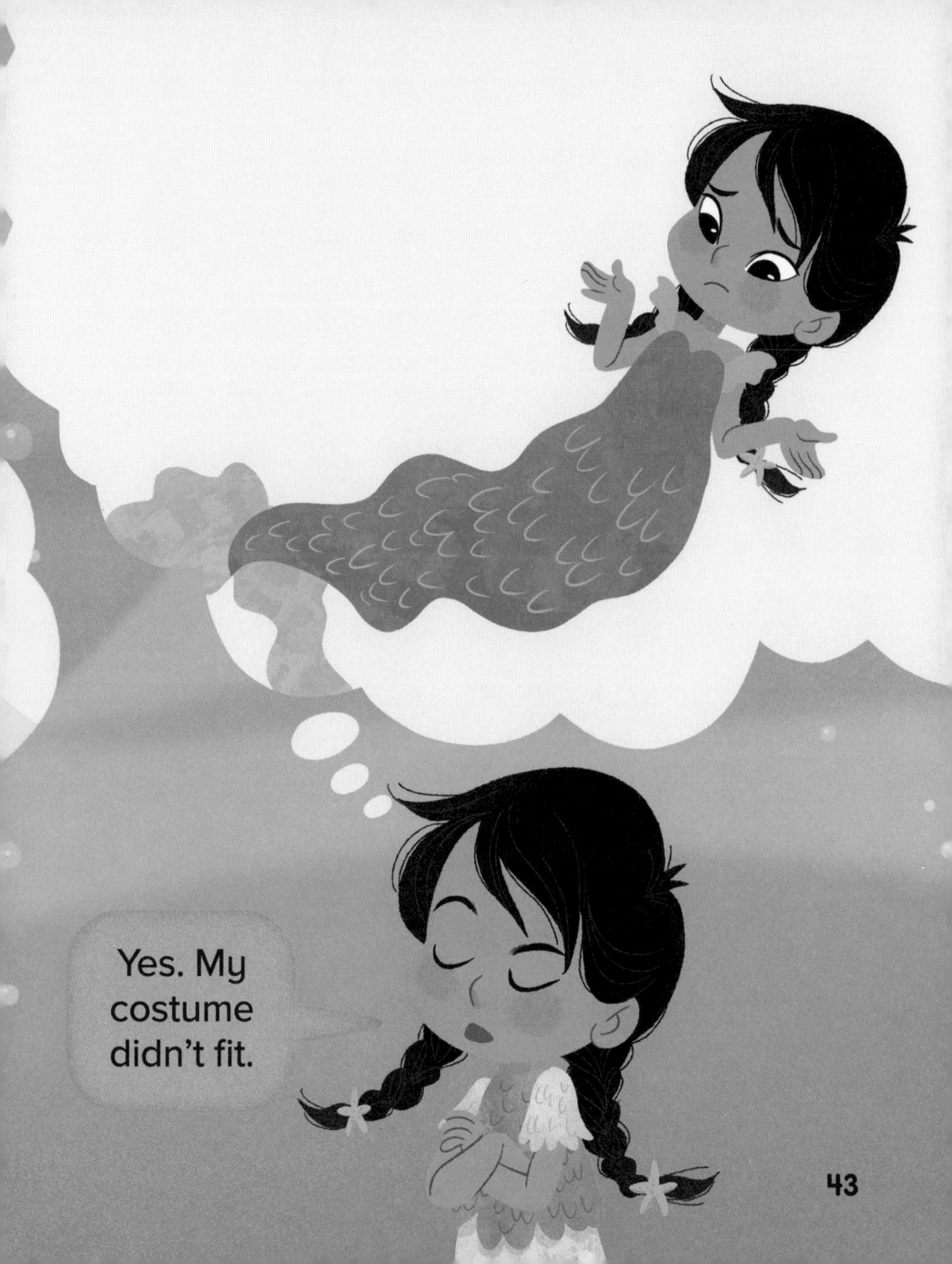
Yes. My costume didn't fit.

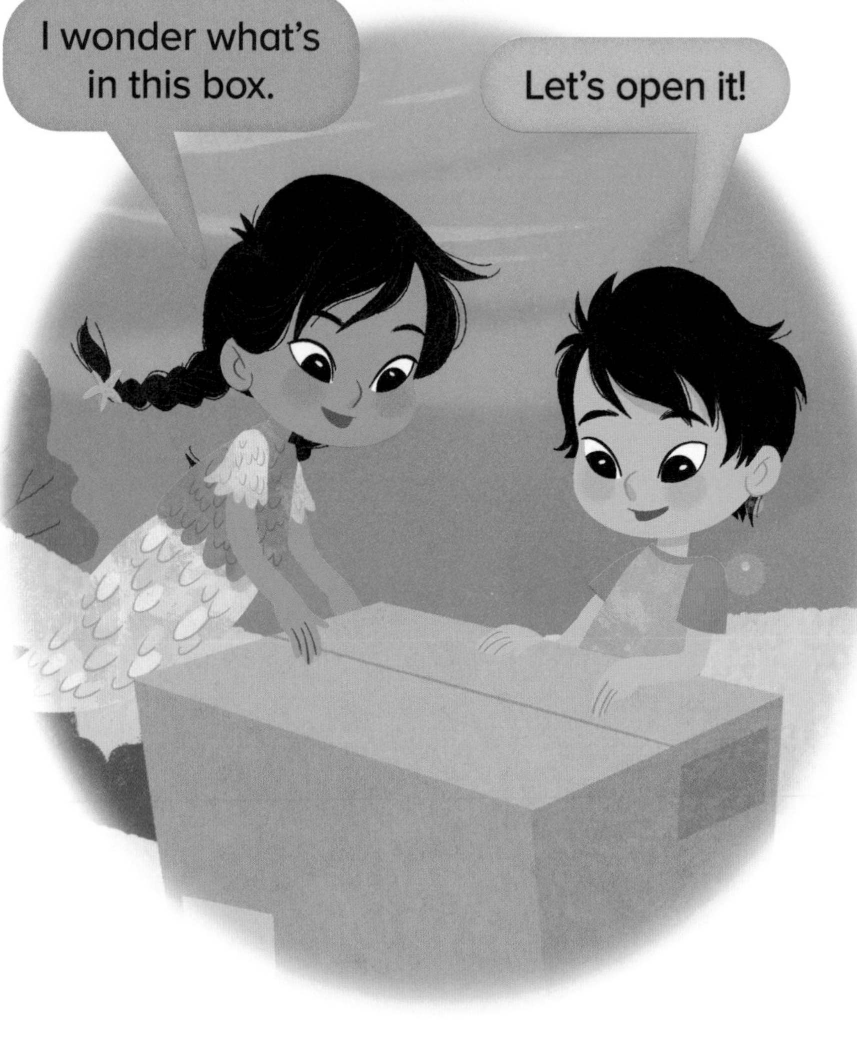
I wonder what's in this box.
Let's open it!

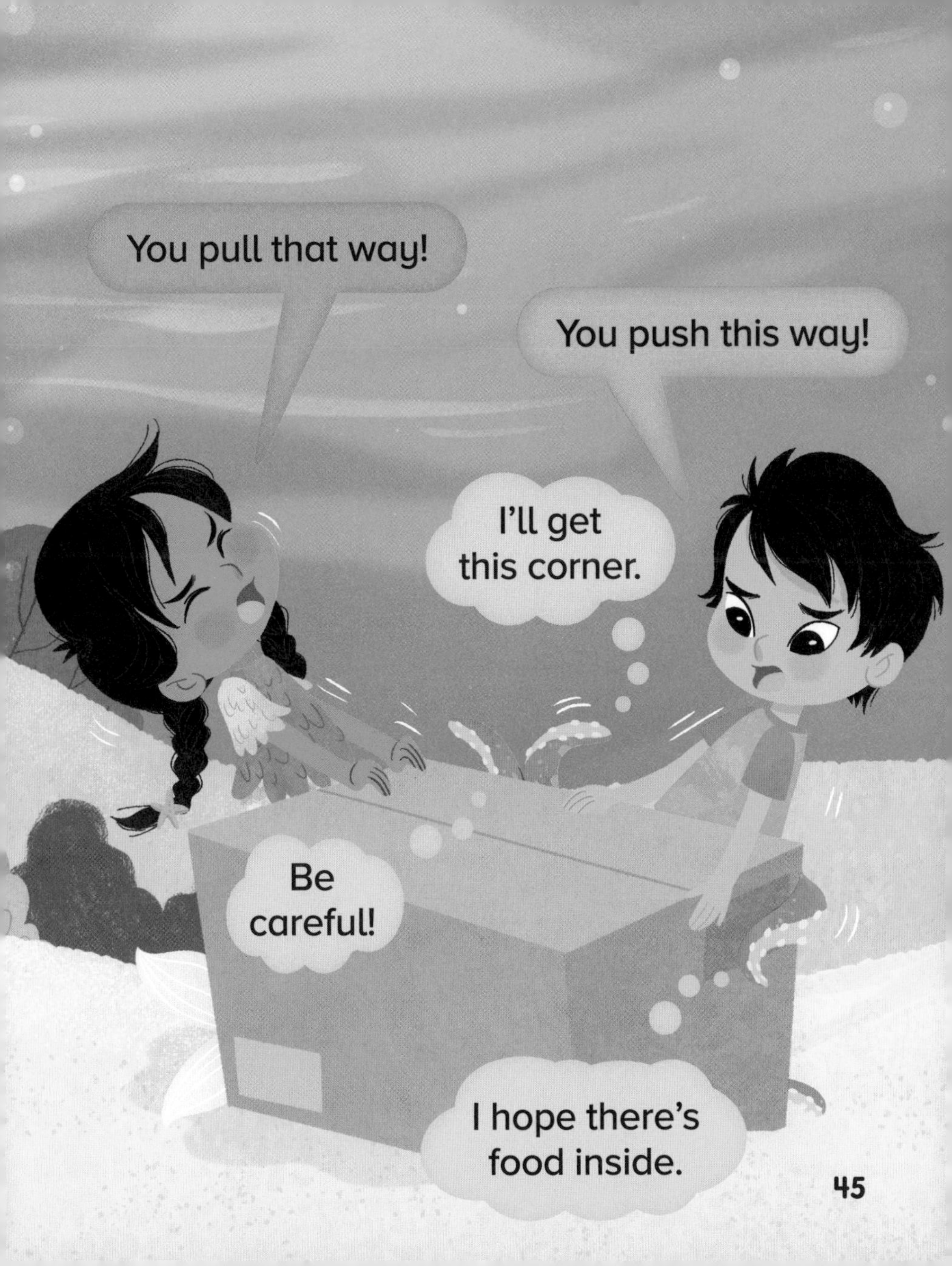
You pull that way!
You push this way!
I'll get this corner.
Be careful!
I hope there's food inside.

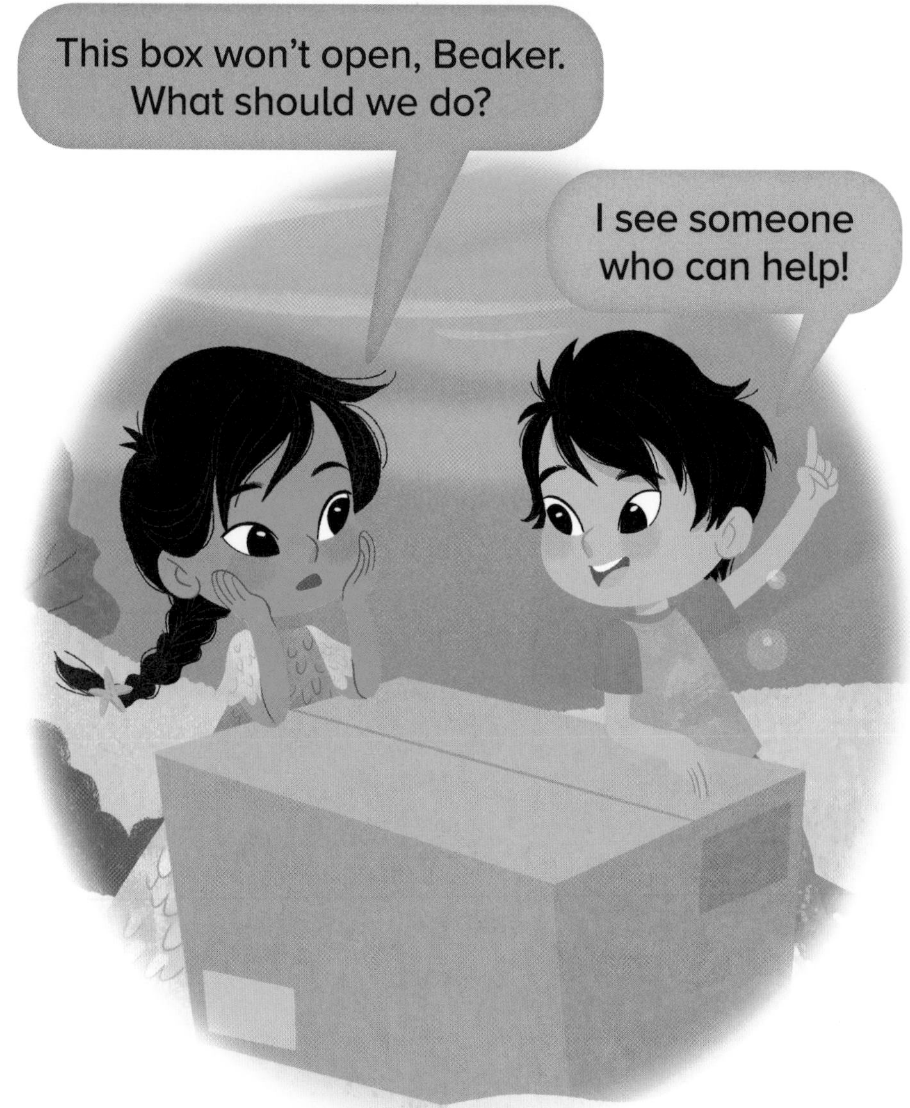
This box won't open, Beaker.
What should we do?
I see someone
who can help!

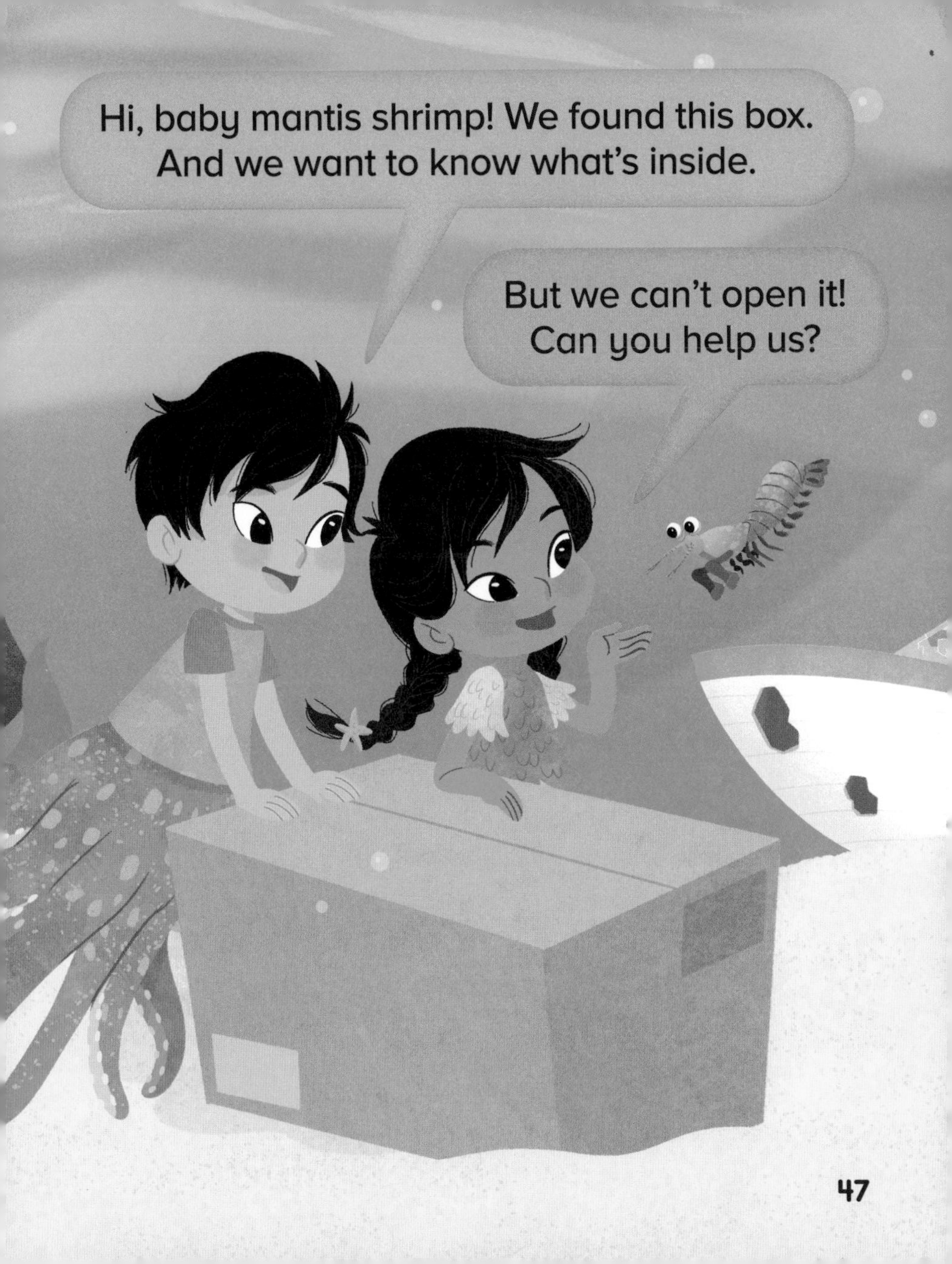
Hi, baby mantis shrimp! We found this box. And we want to know what's inside.
But we can't open it! Can you help us?

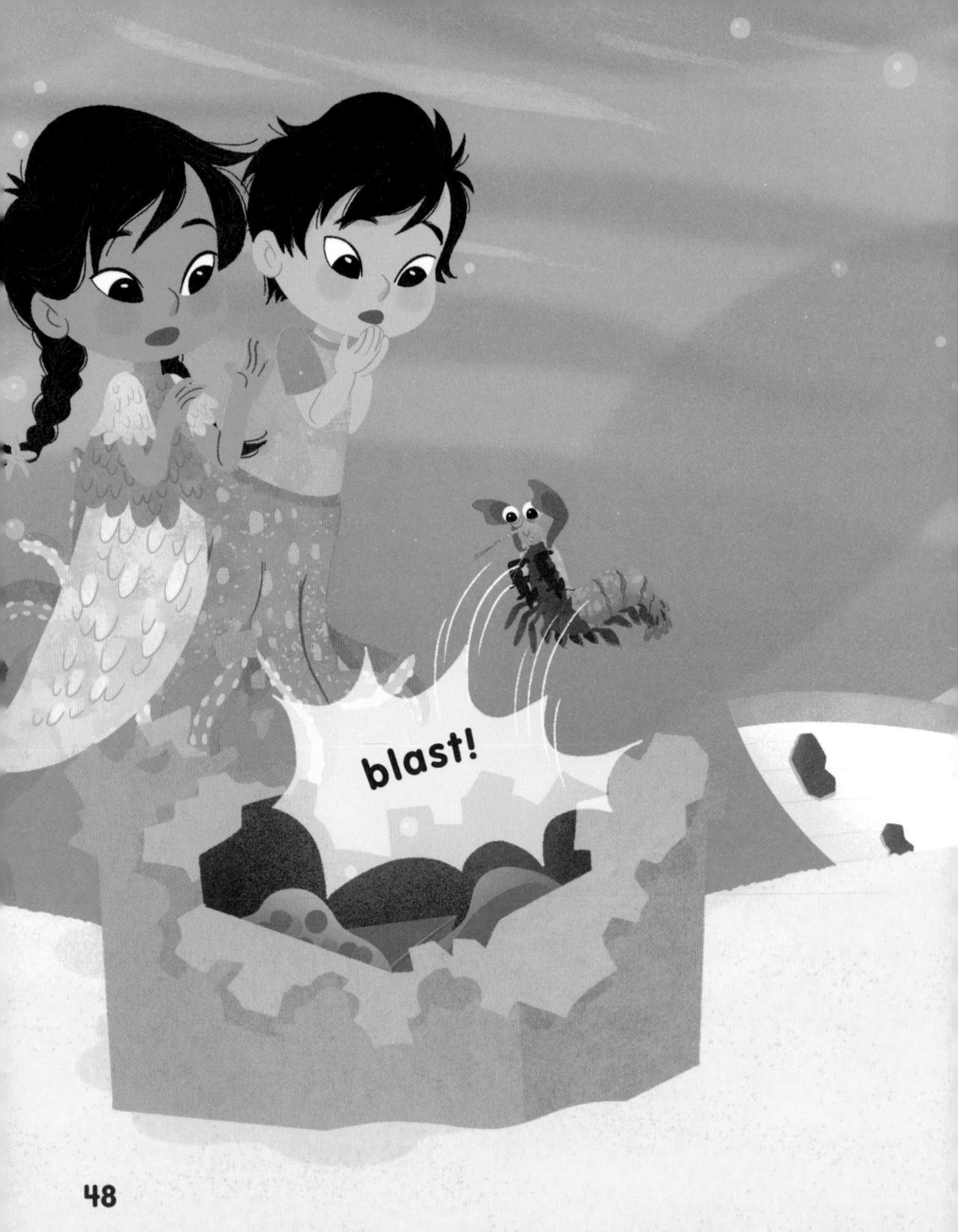
blast!

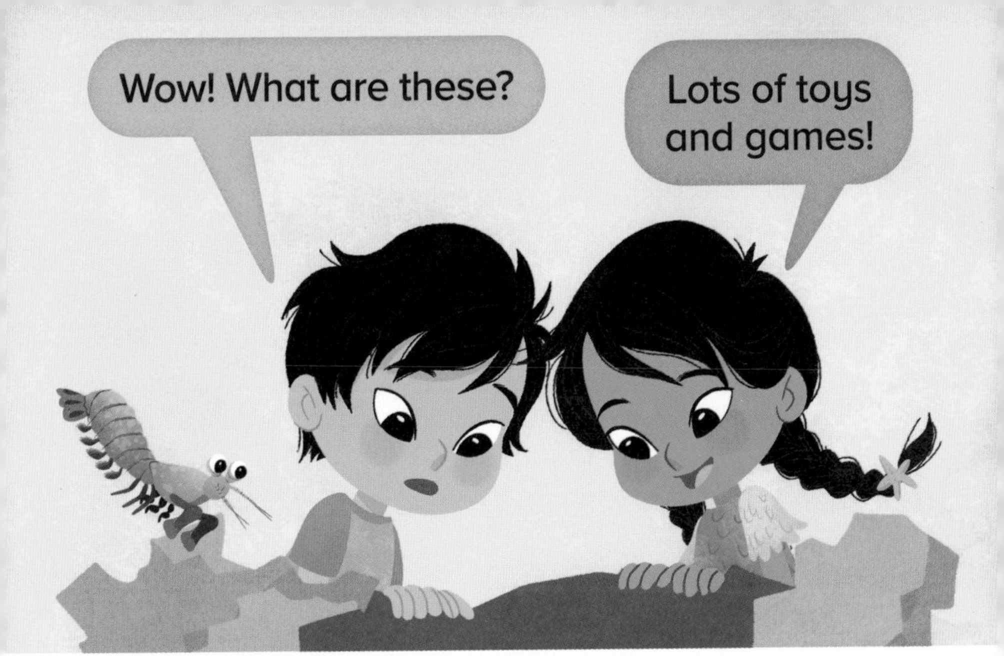
Wow! What are these?
Lots of toys and games!

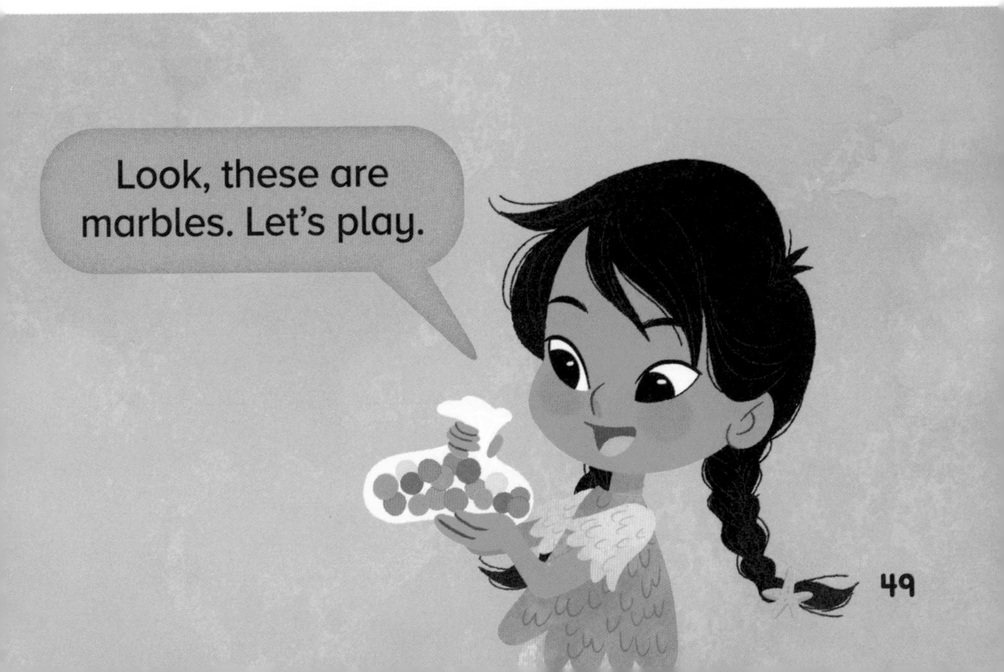
Look, these are marbles. Let's play.

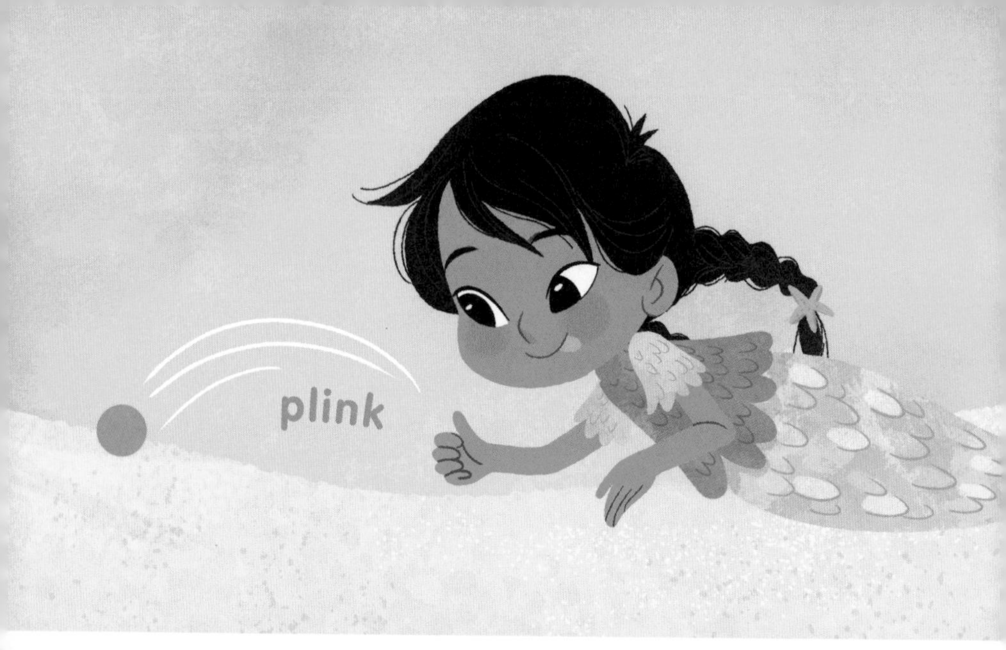
plink

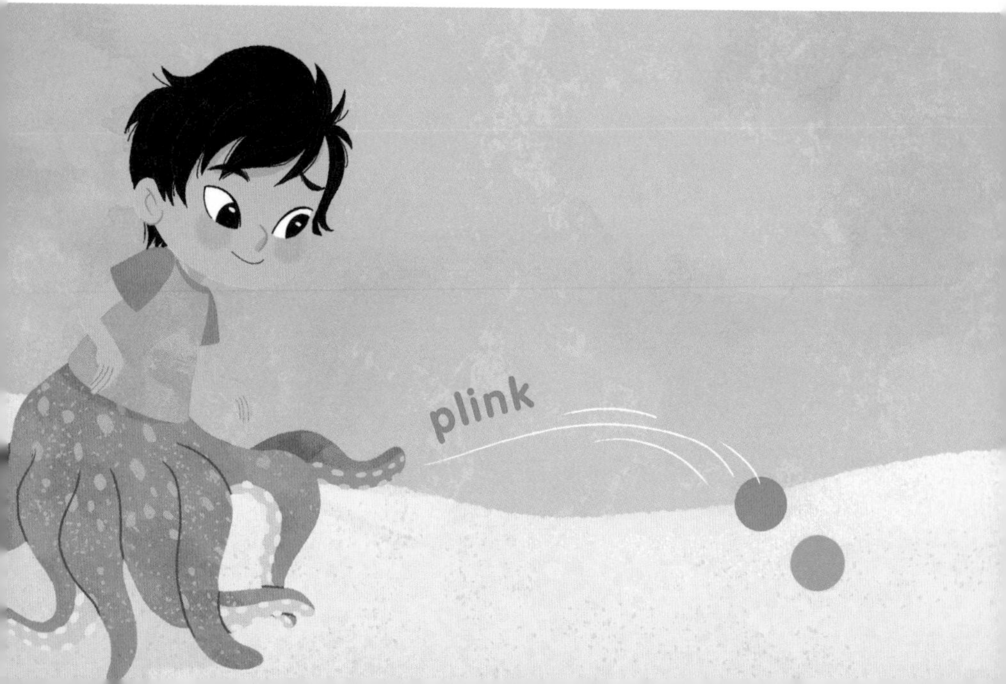
plink

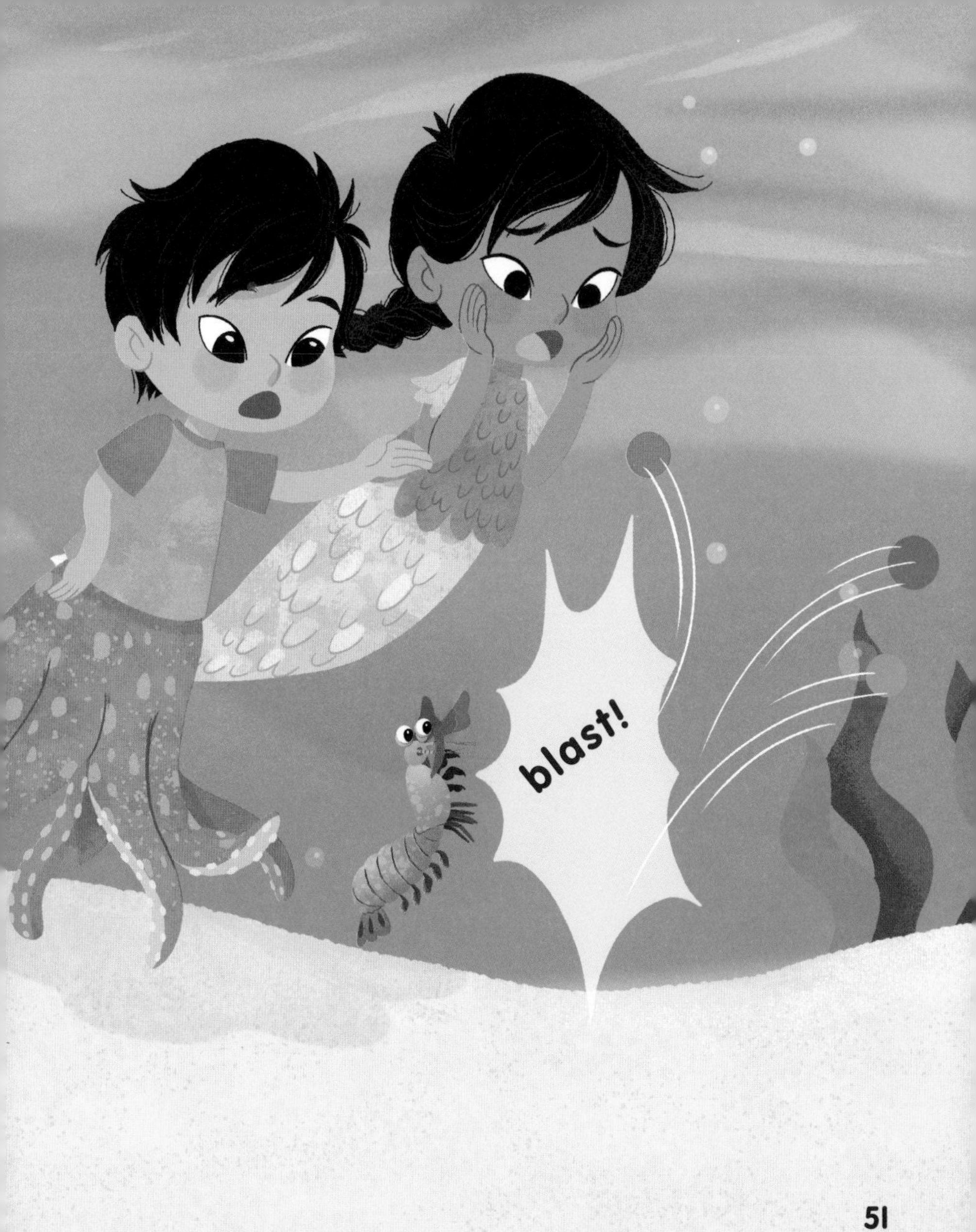
blast!

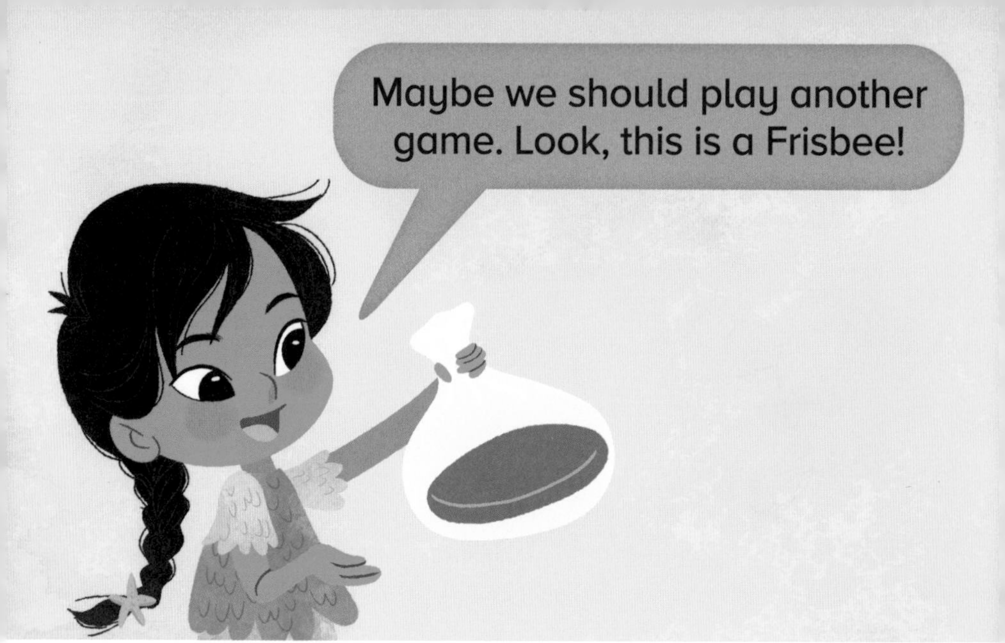
Maybe we should play another game. Look, this is a Frisbee!

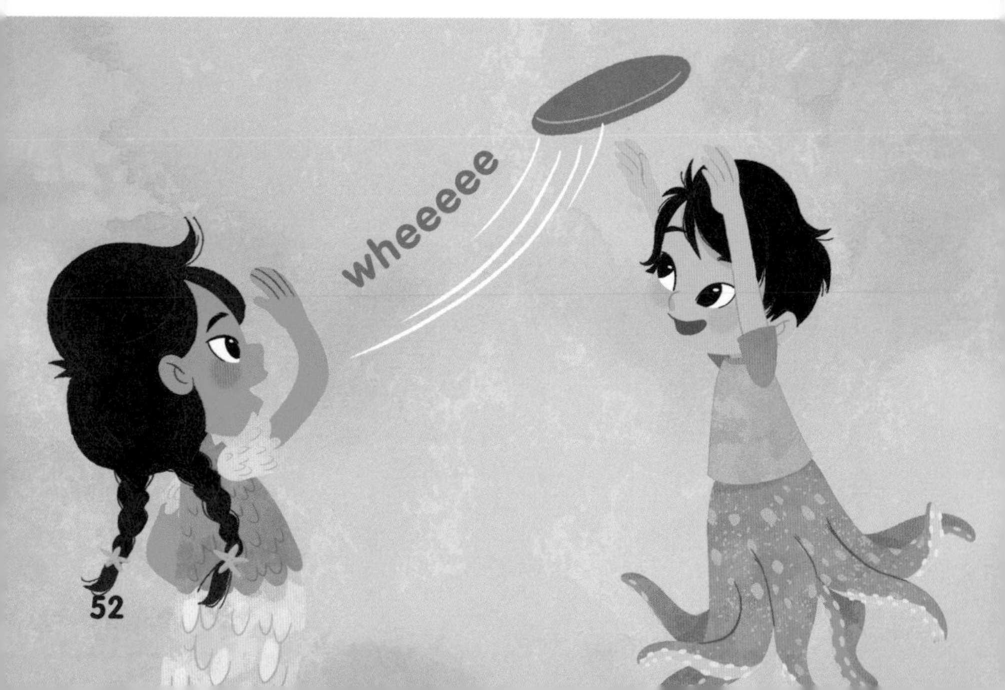
wheeeee

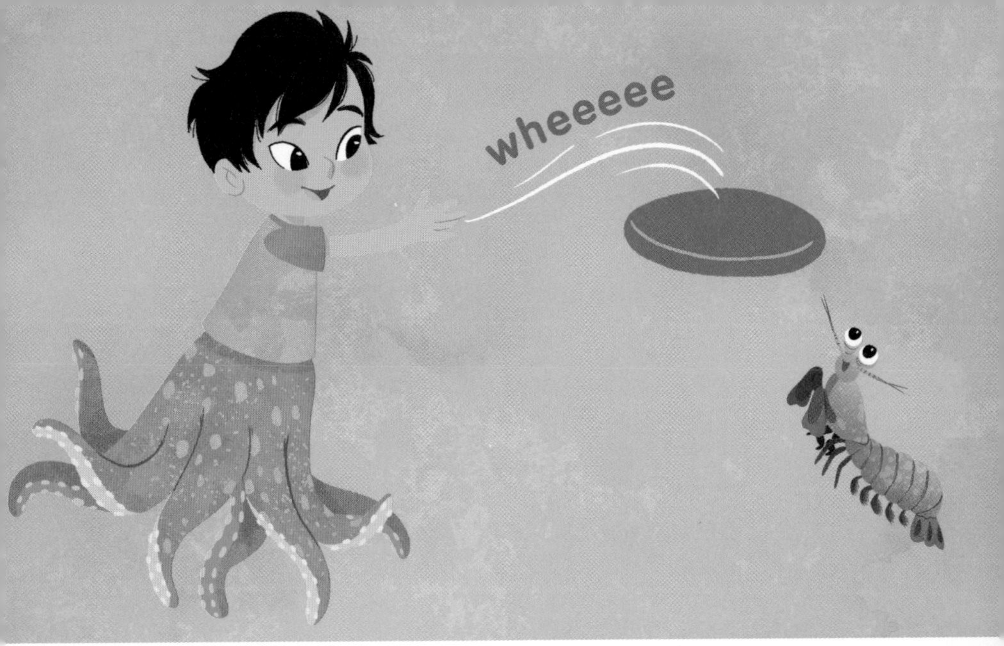
wheeeee

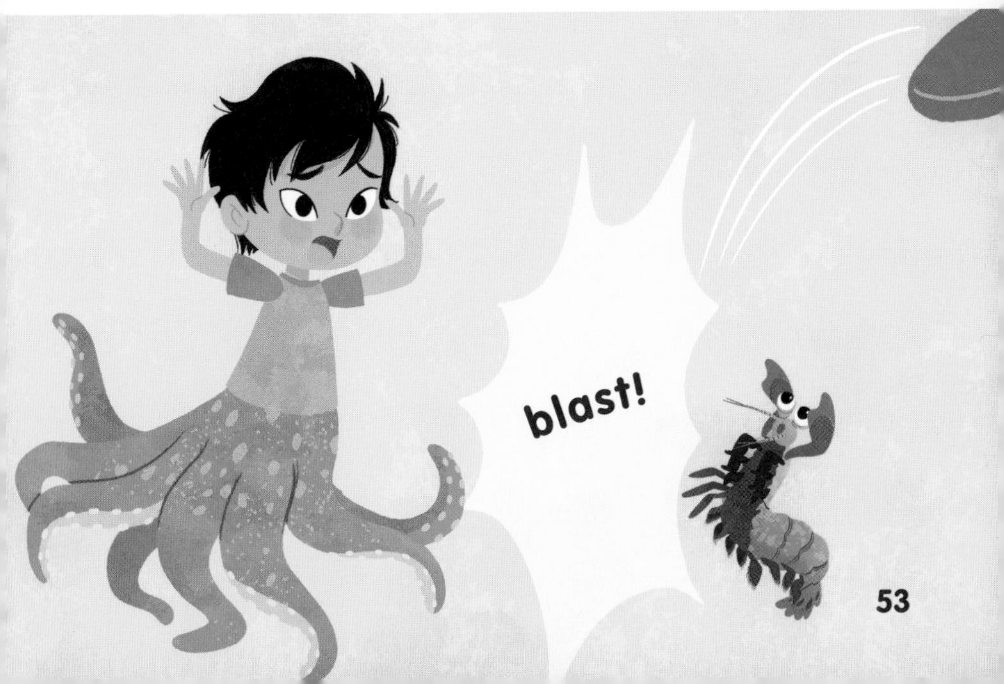
blast!

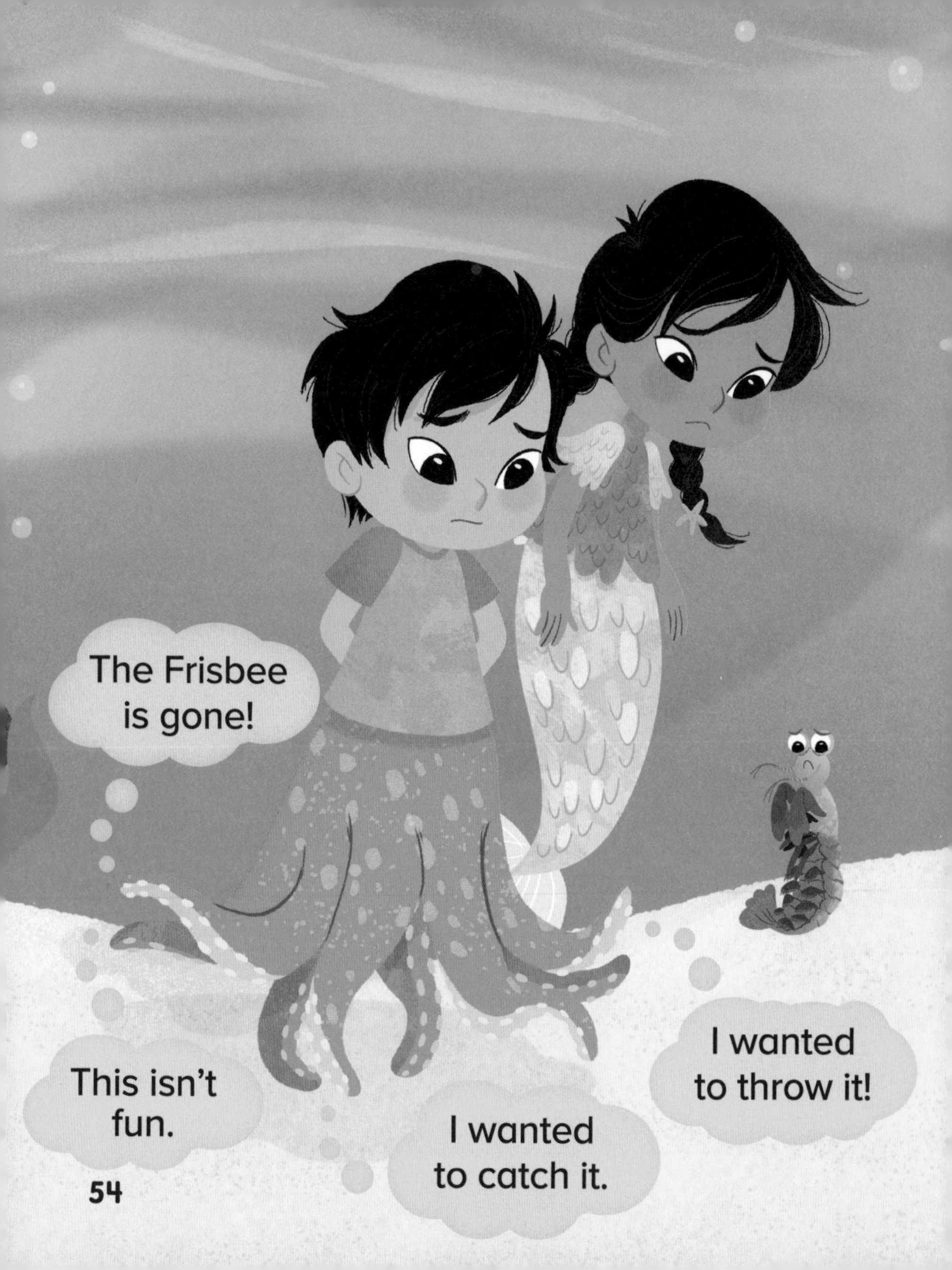
The Frisbee is gone!
This isn't fun.
I wanted to catch it.
I wanted to throw it!

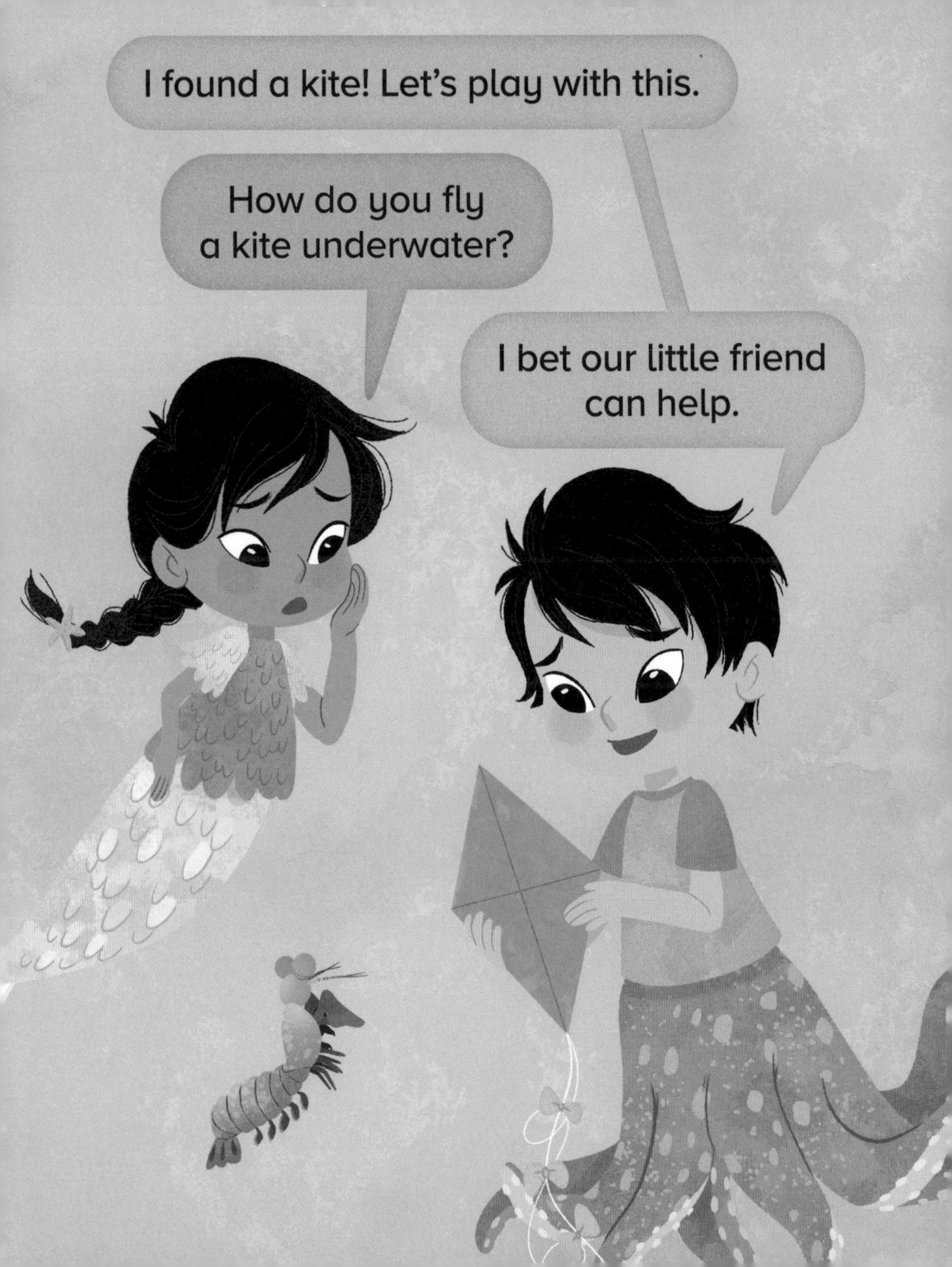

I found a kite! Let's play with this.
How do you fly a kite underwater?
I bet our little friend can help.

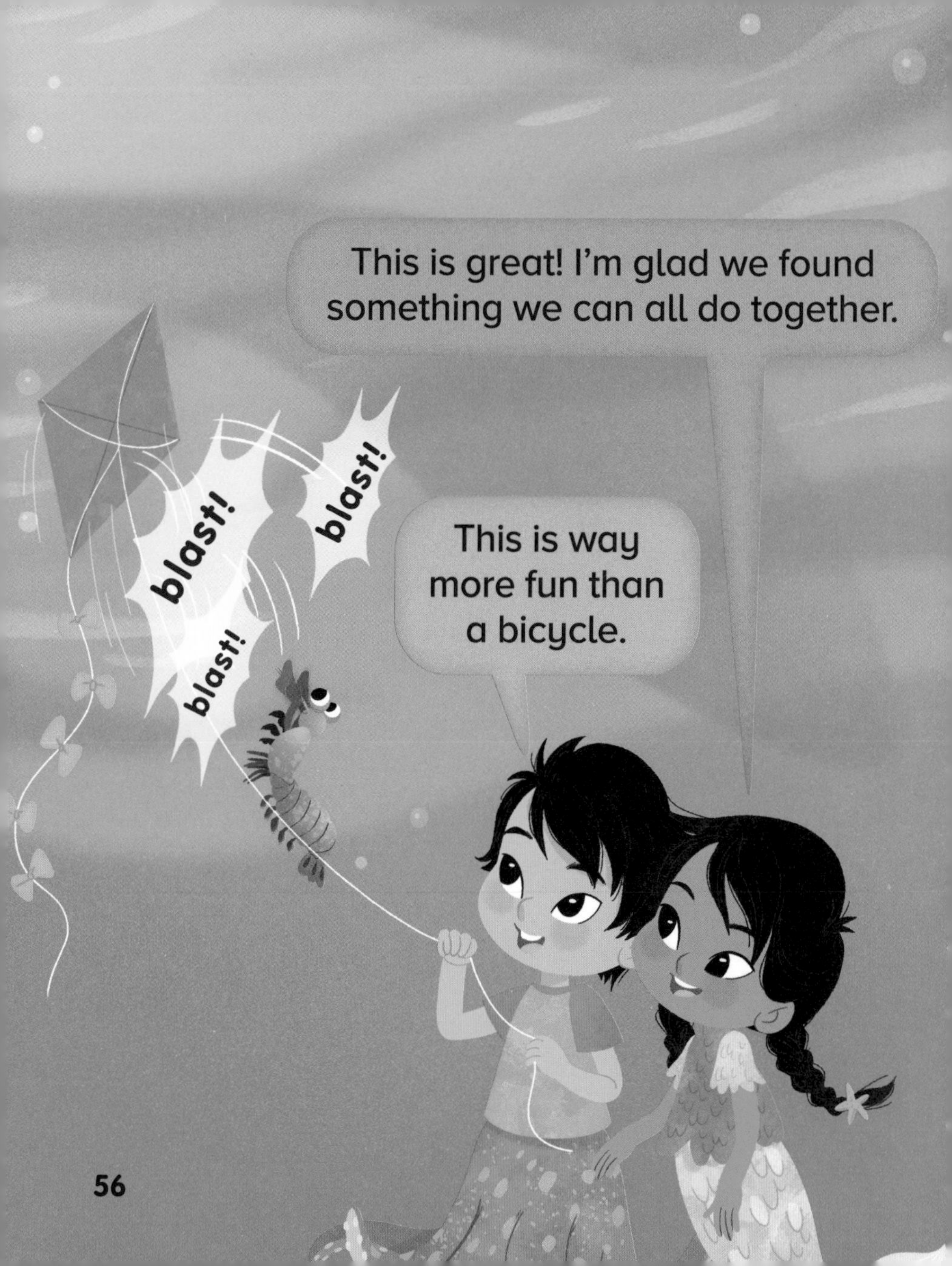

This is great! I'm glad we found something we can all do together.
This is way more fun than a bicycle.
blast!
blast!
blast!

ABOUT THE CREATORS

 **KYLE LUKOFF** has never met a mermaid. He would very much like to be friends with an octopus! But he would rather climb trees than go to the beach, and he would rather write books for kids than learn how to scuba dive. He is a National Book Award finalist and the Newbery and Stonewall award–winning author of lots of books, including WHEN AIDAN BECAME A BROTHER and TOO BRIGHT TO SEE.

 **KAT UNO** was born, raised, and currently resides in Hawaii. Living on an island surrounded by the beautiful Pacific Ocean has always provided much inspiration. Kat has loved being creative ever since she was little. She enjoys illustrating children's books, and mermaids are one of her favorite subjects to draw! She is also a proud mom of two eager readers.

YOU CAN DRAW BEAKER!

1. Draw the outline of Beaker's head, torso, and lower body.

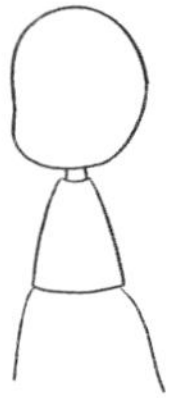

2. Add eight wiggly legs to their lower body.

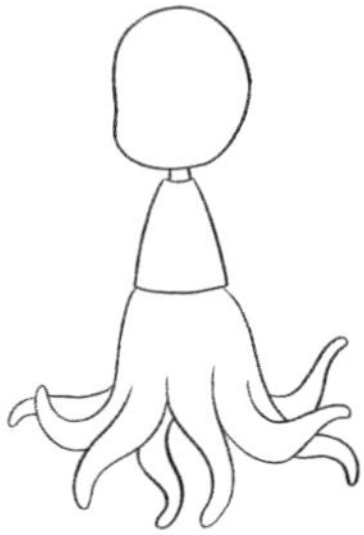

3. Add short sleeves on their shirt and give them two arms and hands.

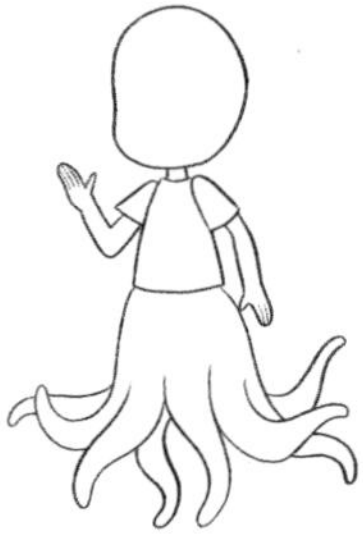

4. Draw their hair. Then give them an ear.

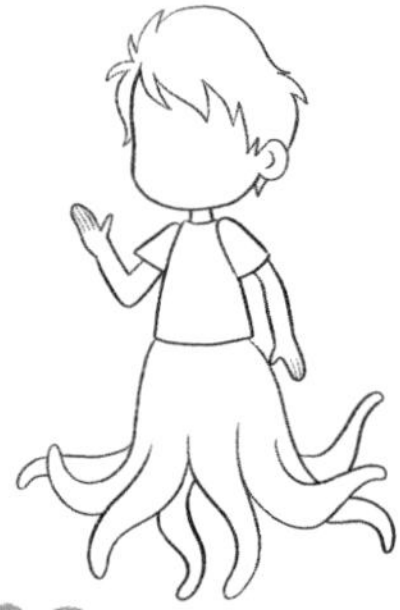

5. Draw Beaker's face and add details to their legs.

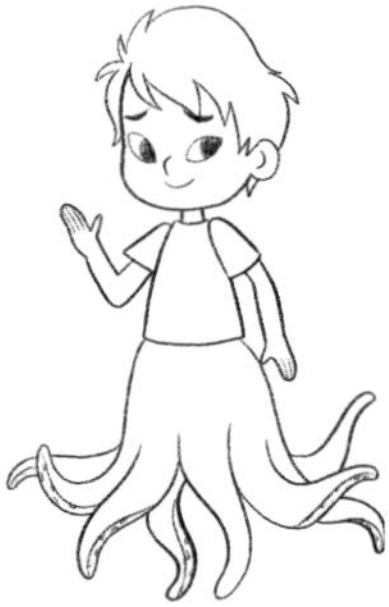

6. Color in your drawing!

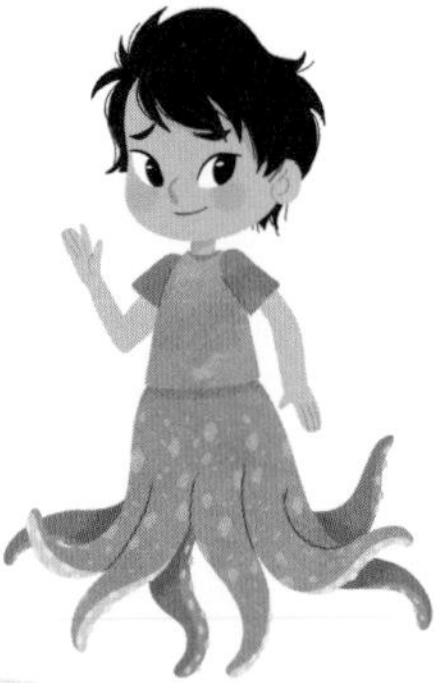

WHAT'S YOUR STORY?

Vera and Beaker meet a baby mantis shrimp.
Imagine that **you** meet a baby mantis shrimp!
What game would you like to play?
How would you play together?
Write and draw your story!

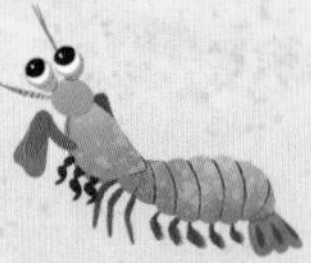